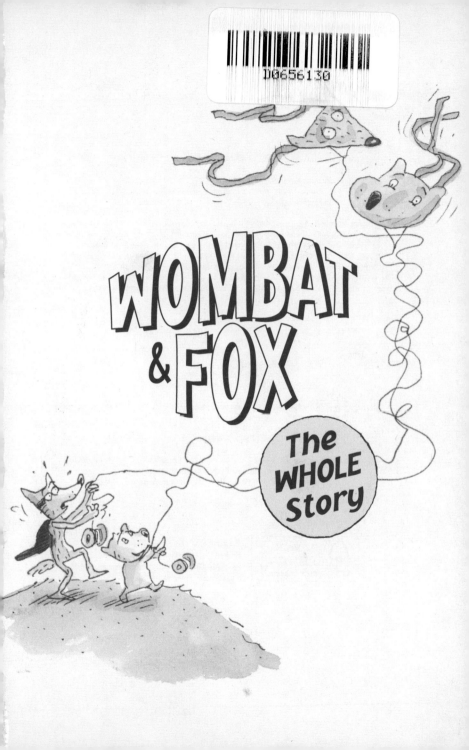

WOMBAT & FOX

The WHOLE Story

This bind-up edition published by Allen & Unwin in 2017

Wombat and Fox: Tales of the City © Terry Denton 2006
Wombat and Fox: Summer in the City © Terry Denton 2007
Wombat and Fox: Thrillseekers © Terry Denton 2009

Allen & Unwin
83 Alexander Street
Crows Nest NSW 2065
Australia
Phone: (61 2) 8425 0100
Email: info@allenandunwin.com
Web: www.allenandunwin.com

A Cataloguing-in-Publication entry is available from the National Library of Australia
www.trove.nla.gov.au

ISBN 978 1 76029 435 9

Cover and text design by Terry Denton, Sandra Nobes and Shahirah Hambali
Set in Bembo by Sandra Nobes
Printed by McPherson's Printing Group, Australia

1 3 5 7 9 10 8 6 4 2

MIX
Paper from
responsible sources
FSC® C001695

The paper in this book is FSC® certified.
FSC® promotes environmentally responsible,
socially beneficial and economically viable
management of the world's forests.

WOMBAT & FOX

The WHOLE Story

TERRY DENTON

ALLEN&UNWIN
SYDNEY · MELBOURNE · AUCKLAND · LONDON

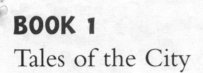

Contents

WOMBAT

Rare yellow urban wombat.
Usually cool, calm and
very stubborn.
Diet: Anything and chips.
Likes: Porridge, Fox.
Dislikes: Rainy days.

FOX

Jumpy, moody and very
emotional masked fox.
Diet: Fussy.
Likes: New capes, Wombat.
Dislikes: The Five Monkeys.

CROC

Fun-seeking slightly
out-of-control reptile.
Diet: Everything.
Likes: Scaring the Five
Monkeys.
Dislikes: Spiders.

THE FIVE MONKEYS

Extremely annoying monkeys
who love annoying Fox.
Diet: Anything
anyone else is eating.
Likes: Annoying Fox.
Dislikes: Croc.

BANDICOOT

Small mouse-like marsupial
[with a built-in wallet] –
the richest fellow in town.
Diet: Oysters in gold sauce.
Likes: Making money.
Hates: Losing money.

THE HIPPO SISTERS

Twin sisters who love
any job that comes
with a uniform.
Diet: Anything, and lots of it.
Likes: Rules.
Dislikes: Rule-breakers.

WOMBAT & FOX
BOOK 1

TALES of the CITY

Wombat's Lucky Dollar

This is a story of what happened to
Wombat on Tuesday. I could tell you
about Monday, but nothing happened
on Monday. So Tuesday it is.

Wombat's phone was nearly out of credit
so he went to the mobile phone shop.
He had never needed to get credit before.
He had no one much to phone.
Except Fox.
Only Fox always had
his phone turned off
to save the battery.

'I would like some
more phone credit,'
said Wombat.
The man behind the counter gave
Wombat a long hard stare. He snorted.

'**How much do
you want to pay?**' he asked.
'Do I have to pay?' said Wombat.

'**Of course you have to pay!**'
'But I don't have anything to pay with,'
said Wombat.

'**No money!
No credit!**'

Wombat sat outside cooling his feet in the
water that was running down the gutter.
'I want to be a millionaire when I grow up,'
he thought.

Speaking of millionaires,
Bandicoot drove by.

He tooted his car horn.
'Hi, Wombat,' he called. 'Guess who just
bought a brand new red sports car?'
Wombat ignored him.
'How come he is a millionaire
and I'm not?' said Wombat.
'Stupid Bandicoot!'
He continued to paddle his feet
in the cool gutter water.

Wombat noticed something
shining in the sunlight.
On the footpath, to his left.

Your right.

His left.

'A coin,' cried Wombat.
'A shiny, new dollar coin!'

He waited.
Just in case whoever dropped it returned.
But no one came.
So Wombat
picked it up.

He used the last of his
phone credit to call Fox.

Fox sat upright in bed.
He coughed and a few feathers flew up.
Chicken feathers, I think!

**'Where's my
stupid phone?'**
he cried.

'Hang on, phone! I'm coming!'

As Fox ran, his big toe
caught in the hem
of his cape and
he tumbled down
the stairs.

He knocked over
the hall table.
The phone bounced
off his head.
Fox caught it.

'Yello!'

he said.

'Wombat?
Why are you ringing me
in the middle of the night?'

'It's midday, Foxy!'

'Oh!' said Fox.

**'Well, that's the middle
of the night for me.'**

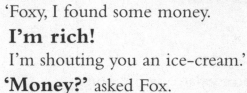

'Foxy, I found some money.

I'm rich!

I'm shouting you an ice-cream.'

'Money?' asked Fox.

'How much money?'

Wombat ignored Fox's question.
'Meet me in the park in ten minutes.'

'I'll have a lemon gelato,' said Wombat.

'What?' said the grumpy man in the ice-cream van.

'A lemon gelato,' said Wombat. 'You have to talk up, Foxy. He doesn't hear well.'

'I'll have a double pistachio and vanilla,' shouted Fox.

Then he remembered it was Wombat's treat.

'Make that a triple!'
'No need to shout,'
shouted the ice-cream vendor.
'That'll be
ten dollars!'

'Oops,' said Wombat. 'I don't have ten dollars.
I only have one dollar.'

'What!' yelled the ice-cream vendor.
'Thieving animals!
Give back my ice-creams!'

Fox panicked.
His hand trembled so much that he
dropped his triple pistachio and vanilla.

'Let's get out of here,' said Wombat.
He and Fox ran along the path,
took a short cut through
the bushes and hid
under a bridge.

'Is he gone?' whispered Fox.
'Think so!' said Wombat.

The two friends huddled under
the bridge and watched the ducks
and swans swimming on the lake.

Wombat licked his ice-cream.
'Want some, Foxy?'

'I hate lemon gelato,' said Fox.
'I love it,' said another voice. 'I want a lick.'

It was Water Rat in a canoe in the reeds
beside the bridge.

He tried to snatch
the ice-cream.
Wombat pulled
it out of reach.

'**RAT!!**' cried Fox.

He jumped up,
and banged his head
on the underside
of the bridge.

'Ouch!'

Fox saw stars and
sat down again.

'You want my ice-cream?' asked Wombat.
'Let's trade.'
'No,' said Water Rat,
snatching at the
ice-cream again.

Wombat smacked him
hard on the hand.

'Ooowww!'
cried Water Rat.
'Don't hit.'

Wombat saw the
angry ice-cream vendor
hurrying towards the bridge.

'Here's the deal,'
he said to Water Rat,
'You give us a go in
your canoe and
you can have a lick
of my ice-cream.'

'A go for a lick? **No deal,**'
said Water Rat. 'You must think I'm stupid.'

The ice-cream vendor stood on the bridge
and looked around.

'What about
the whole ice-cream?'
said Wombat.
'Maybe,'
said Water Rat.
'Okay, how about the ice-cream
and my lucky dollar coin?' said Wombat.

'Deal,' said Water Rat.

Water Rat stepped out of the canoe.
Wombat passed the ice-cream
and the coin to him.
Wombat and Fox climbed into the canoe
and quickly paddled out on the lake.

'This is no dollar coin!'
shouted Water Rat.

He threw the coin at Wombat.
Wombat ducked and the coin hit Fox instead.

Right on the end of his nose.

The coin dropped at Wombat's feet.
He picked it up
and popped it in his pocket.

'Stop, thieves!'
shouted the ice-cream vendor.

Wombat and Fox paddled
across the lake.
'Paddle faster,
Foxy,' said
Wombat.

Water Rat and
the ice-cream
vendor ran as
fast as they
could around
the lake.

As the canoe neared the other side,
Wombat handed Fox a rope.
'Guide us ashore, Foxy.'

Fox stood up. His cape billowed in the wind.
Everybody watching asked,
'Who is that mysterious masked fox?'
Or so Fox imagined.

The canoe ran aground. Fox fell forward into
the water and got thoroughly drenched.

'My cape is ruined!' he cried.
Wombat fetched Fox out of the water.
'Let's get out of here, Foxy,' he said.
They ran across the lawn.

The Hippo Sisters stood by their tandem
bicycle, thinking. They were always
thinking about going for a ride.

'Can we borrow your
tandem?' asked Wombat.
'No,' said the Sisters.
'Wombat has a lucky dollar,' said Fox.
'If you let us borrow the bike,
you can have the dollar.'
'Show us,' they said.

The Hippo Sisters looked at the coin.
'That's not even a dollar,' they cried.
They threw it back at Wombat.

Wombat ducked and the coin bounced off Fox's head. Wombat picked it up. 'It keeps coming back,' he said. 'Maybe it *really is* a lucky dollar.'

The ice-cream vendor and Water Rat ran across the lawn towards Wombat and Fox. **'Come on, Foxy,'** said Wombat. They jumped on the tandem and pedalled away. 'Come back with our bike,' the Sisters cried.

Wombat and Fox
wobbled
onto the path.

Then off the path.

Then across the path.

'I've never ridden
one of these before,' cried Fox.
'Me neither,' said Wombat.
'Head for the gates,' said Fox.
'I'll follow you.'

People and animals and swans and ducks
scattered in all directions. As Wombat and
Fox passed through the gates, a lady with a
pram stepped out in front of them.
She screamed.
Wombat slammed on the brakes.

The bike stopped.

But Fox kept going.

Over Wombat.
Over the pram lady.

Onto the grass.

Wombat
landed
on top of Fox.

'*Ha ha ha!*'

said Bandicoot, leaning
on his shiny red sports car.

'Bandicoot!' said Wombat.
'We need to borrow your car.'

'Now, why would I
lend you my
brand new sports car, Wombat?'
asked Bandicoot.
'He'll give you
his lucky
dollar coin
if you do,'
said Fox.

The angry ice-cream vendor,
Water Rat and the Hippo Sisters
all ran towards the gates.

Bandicoot took out
a small eyepiece
and examined
Wombat's coin.
**'Hurry up,
Bandicoot!'**
said Wombat.

'Okay, my friend,'
said Bandicoot.
'You have a deal.'
Bandicoot pocketed
the coin and
Wombat and Fox
jumped into his car.
They drove off
just in the
nick of time.

'At last we
got rid of that
stupid coin,' cried Fox.
'That was my lucky dollar,'
said Wombat.
'Some luck,' said Fox.
'Since you found that coin,
I've fallen down stairs, lost a triple
pistachio and vanilla ice-cream, nearly
drowned in a lake, ruined my cape and
fallen off a bicycle. **That's the *unluckiest***
coin in the universe!'

'Where are
you going,
Wombat?'

They drove through a red light and
down a one-way street.

'Turn left!' shouted Fox.

Wombat turned right.

Your left.

His right.

'Wombat, do you know
how to drive?'

'No,' said Wombat.

'Stop
the car!'
yelled Fox.

'I'm driving.'

The car lurched
forward and kangaroo-
hopped along the road.

It mounted the kerb
and bumped into
a palm tree.

'You can't drive either!' said Wombat.
'I'm better than you!' yelled Fox.
'At least I stayed on the road!'
said Wombat.
'You drove through

a red light,'
yelled Fox.

'Hello,' said a familiar voice.
It was Croc, out for an afternoon walk.
'Croc, can you drive?' asked Wombat.
'Sure can,' she said. 'Shove over, Fox.'

Croc was a good driver compared
to Wombat and Fox.
She drove down the Boulevard,
the wrong way round
a roundabout

and through
a floral clock.

She almost ran over a police officer,

two dogs

and the lady with the pram.

'Good driving, Croc,' said Wombat.
'Let's go sight-seeing,' suggested Croc.
They drove to the
Town Hall and listened
to the clock strike
three.

At the
Power Station
they watched
the steam clouds
billowing out
of the
chimneys.

Then they drove to the 24-hour
concrete crushing
plant.

Finally they drove
to Stop River,
under the Big Bridge.
The sign at the end of the road said,

'STOP
RIVER.'

They looked up at the Big Bridge.
They listened to the traffic noises.
And counted trucks.
'...112, 113, 114, 115,' said Fox.
Wombat and Croc soon became
bored with truck-counting.

'Where is the car?' asked Wombat.

'Did you put the handbrake
on, Croc?' cried Fox.
'What's a handbrake?'
asked Croc.
They found Bandicoot's car
floating in Stop River.

'It must have rolled in,' said Wombat.
'I can't believe we didn't see it rolling,'
said Croc.
**'I can't believe
you didn't put
the handbrake
on,'** yelled Fox.
**'What's a
handbrake?'**
asked Croc.

Then a big ship cruised by,
and pushed Bandicoot's car
even deeper into Stop River.

'We'd better tell Bandicoot,' said Wombat.
'He'll sell us into slavery,' said Fox.
'He'll turn me into suitcases,' said Croc.

They trudged back along the Boulevard
to Bandicoot's place.
Wombat knocked
on the door.

'Am I glad to see you!' said Bandicoot.
'Did you enjoy driving my new
shiny red sports car, Wombat?'
'Yes, but–' said Wombat.
Bandicoot held up his hand.
'Wait,' he said.
'I have a surprise.'

'You know that coin you gave me, Wombat?'
'My lucky dollar?' said Wombat.
'The *unluckiest* coin in the world,'
added Fox.
'It wasn't a dollar coin at all,' said Bandicoot.
'It was a rare Transylvanian Tuppence.
And it's worth a fortune.'

'Oh,' said Wombat.

'Two fortunes in fact,' added Bandicoot.

'Oh,' said Fox.

'I am an even richer man now,'
said Bandicoot. 'So I want to reward you,
Wombat. You can keep my new shiny
red sports car. **It's all yours!'**

'Oh,' said Croc.

Wombat, Fox and Croc walked down
the Boulevard towards Fox's place.
Nobody said anything.

There was
nothing
to say.

Goldenboot Fox

Wombat loves Wednesdays. That's because Wednesday starts with a 'W'– Wombat's favourite letter of the alphabet.

On Wednesday, Wombat, Fox and Croc were practising goal-kicking in the park behind the Oldmeadow building.

Wombat and Croc were
very good at kicking goals.
But Fox wasn't.
In fact, he was hopeless.

'Try again, Foxy,' Wombat said.
'Just relax!'
'Relax?' said Fox.
'I have tried 123 times to kick a goal.
And 123 times I have missed.
How can I relax?'

Fox prepared himself for attempt number 124.
He took a deep breath.
He stared at the very centre of the goal
and then he looked back at the ball.

Five steps back.
Five steps forward.
Fox kicked.

The ball flew towards the net, but at the last
moment it flew high over the
top bar of the goal.

Fox sank to his knees.
'NNNOOO! That's 124 misses in a row,'
he cried. 'I'll never get the ball in the net.'
'Yes, you will, Foxy,' said Wombat.
'Just keep trying.'
So Fox tried again.

'Number 125,' said Fox.
He kicked. He missed.
'And another thing,' said Wombat.
'Stop counting each attempt!'

'Maybe he has crooked feet,' said Croc.
'Don't be ridiculous,' said Fox.
'My feet aren't crooked!'
Croc and Wombat
studied Fox's feet.

'Maybe you're right, Croc,' said Wombat.
'They do look crooked.'
'Yes,' Croc agreed.
'The right one
curves inwards
and the left one
is pointing towards
the rubbish bin.'

'My feet aren't crooked!' cried Fox.
'I think Croc might be right,' said Wombat.
'You can't kick goals with crooked feet, Fox,'
said Croc.

'Enough of this rubbish,' said Fox.
He stormed back to the kick-off spot.

'Hey! Where's the ball?' asked Fox.

'Are you looking for this?'
It was the Five Monkeys.
They all laughed as the
oldest monkey
held up
Fox's ball.

He passed it to the second-oldest monkey,
who passed it to the middle monkey.

And they played the ball between themselves.

Around and around Fox.

And then
the youngest
monkey
kicked a goal.

Then the Five Monkeys ran off with the ball.
'Where are you going with my ball?'
cried Fox. Wombat, Fox and Croc chased
the Five Monkeys through the park.

Croc, Fox and Wombat finally caught up
with the Five Monkeys at the playground.
They were standing on the fort.

'Give Fox's ball back,' said Wombat.
'No way,' said the Five Monkeys.
Fox stood on the seesaw
near the fort.

'Give me back my ball, or else!' he cried.
'Or else what?' said the Five Monkeys.
Fox didn't have an answer.

The Five Monkeys
laughed at Fox. Then
they jumped off the
fort onto the other
end of the seesaw.

Fox flew up
into a very
tall tree.

He flew right up
to the top branches,
then fell back
down
through the tree.

'Watch out!'
squawked a bird
in a nest.

'I can't stop!'
cried Fox.

He crashed
through the bird's
nest, destroying
it entirely.
Three baby
birds tumbled
out of the nest.

Wombat and Croc stood
at the base of the tree
waiting to catch Fox,
but when they saw the
baby birds falling, they
ran to catch them instead.

Nobody caught Fox.

'NNNNOOO!'

screamed Fox, as he
crashed to the ground.

Wombat and Croc returned the baby birds
to their parents. At first they were very
relieved to have their babies back.

Then they turned on Fox.
'What do you mean by jumping through
our nest, you crazy fox?' they cried.
'We're ringing the police.'
The mother bird took out her mobile phone.

'Don't do that,' cried Fox. 'It was an
accident. The Five Monkeys are to blame.'

The bird started dialling.
'Stop!' cried Fox. 'What
if I find you a new nest?'

The bird closed up her phone.
'That sounds fair,' she said.

Wombat, Fox and Croc hurried off along the
Boulevard and turned down Celestial Avenue.
'This is serious, Wombat,' said Fox.
'Where are we going to find a nest?'

Under the overhead bridge
they met the Hippo Sisters.
'What are you doing?'
Wombat asked them.
'We're going to the
Boulevard to ride around
the roundabout,' said the
bigger of the Hippo Sisters.

'Yesterday we rode around
it 143 times,' her sister added.
'Till we got so dizzy we fell off our bike.'
'Tonight, we are trying to break that record,'
said the bigger Hippo Sister.
'Why don't you come and cheer us on?'
'I might,' said Croc. 'If I can have a go, too.'

'We can't,' said Wombat.
'We have to find a nest for some birds.'
'Fox wrecked their old one,' Croc added.
'Why would you do that, Fox?'
asked the Hippo Sisters.
'It was an accident,' Fox protested.
'It was the Five Monkeys' fault!'

'Do you know where we can buy a nest?'
Wombat asked.
'Try the second-hand shop on Tin Pot Alley,'
the bigger Hippo Sister suggested.

Wombat, Fox and Croc walked down
Tin Pot Alley to the second-hand shop.
'This is cool,' said Croc. 'It's full
of interesting stuff I need.'

Fox found a soccer ball.
'Ha!' he said, 'This ball is
better than the one the
Five Monkeys stole.'

'Look, Foxy,' said Wombat, holding up some golden boots. 'These might be just what you need to help you kick straight.'

Fox tried on the golden boots and they fitted perfectly. He practised kicking with them.
'I don't think I need them,' he said.
'What we *need* is a replacement nest,' said Wombat.

'What about up there?' said Croc, pointing to an old letterbox. 'It looks just like a little house and it's got a round door.'
'Clever Croc,' said Wombat. 'It's perfect.'

Wombat went to the counter.
'Can you help me, please?' he asked.
'No,' said the shop owner.
'I'm too busy.'
'But I can't reach
the letterbox,' said Wombat.
'I told you I'm busy,'
snapped the owner.
'Help yourself.'

'Well, that's not
very friendly,'
muttered Wombat.

'Foxy, can you give me a hand?'
Fox lifted Wombat up on his shoulders.
'I still can't reach the letterbox,' said Wombat.
So Fox asked Croc for help.

Croc lifted Fox up
on her shoulders and
Wombat balanced
on Fox's shoulders.
Wombat reached out for
the letterbox on the
top shelf.

Fox started to wobble.
'You are very heavy, Wombat,' he said.
Then Croc started to wobble, too.
'You are both very heavy,' she said.

Wombat toppled forward.
Fox staggered back.
Croc's knees began to buckle.

And they all fell down.

Wombat caught hold of the top shelf
as he fell, pulling it forward.
Everything fell off the shelf.
And then the whole shelf fell over.

The shop owner ran
towards them shouting,
'Get out! Get out!
You're wrecking my shop!'
She swiped at them
with a broom.

Wombat, Fox and Croc ran out of the shop
and down the street as fast as their legs
could carry them.

They hid under the railway overpass until it was safe to come out again.

'Are you hurt, Wombat?'
asked Croc.
'No, I'm okay,' said Wombat.
'What about you?'
'I'm fine,' said Croc. 'And
look what I ended up with.'
She was holding up the
second-hand soccer ball.

'I am NOT okay,' said Fox.
He was in a terrible state.
The letterbox was stuck on his head.
'Clever Fox,' said Wombat.
'You've got the birds' new nest.'
'Get this thing off my head,' said Fox.

Wombat and Croc pulled

and pulled

and pulled,

but they couldn't
remove the letterbox
from Fox's head.

Just at that moment Bandicoot drove by.
'Hello, Wombat,' he said. 'Is that Fox in
trouble again?'
'Yes, Bandicoot,' said Wombat. 'He's got
a letterbox stuck on his head and
we can't get it off.'

'You need something
greasy,' said Bandicoot.
'I have something in the
car that might help.'

'Here, Wombat, try this,'
said Bandicoot. 'It's my new
invention, super-greasy triple-
strength hair gel.
It's made me even richer
than I was before.'

Wombat squirted the entire
tube of hair gel through the
letterbox onto Fox's head.

Then he and Croc pulled
on the letterbox.

It popped off easily.

'Thank goodness for that,' said Fox,
rubbing his head all over.

'Well,' said Bandicoot. 'I must go and make some more money.'
'Thank you, Bandicoot,' said Wombat.
'Oh, by the way, Wombat, you owe me twelve dollars for the hair gel.'
'But I don't have twelve dollars,' said Wombat.
'That's okay,' said Bandicoot.
'You can pay me later.'

And he hopped into his car and drove off.

Wombat, Fox and Croc walked back to the soccer field.

Fox took the letterbox
over to the birds.
'Here's your new nest,'
said Fox.
'Thank you,' said the father
bird. 'It's a very fine nest.'

Fox placed the letterbox
in the tree.
'A bit higher,' said the
mother bird.

Then she took Fox by the hand.
'To show all is forgiven you must
share a meal with us, Fox,' she said.
'Oh, no thanks,' said Fox.
'I'm a very fussy eater.'
'But I insist,' said the mother bird.

Fox knew he
had no choice.

The birds served him
their favourite meal
– fresh worms!
Poor Fox had to
eat six worms.
And then a few
beetles for dessert.

After the meal, Fox joined Wombat
and Croc on the soccer field.

'I don't feel so well,'
said Fox.
'Maybe you've had
enough soccer for
one day,' said Wombat.
'We can practise
another day.'
'Yeah, let's watch
the Hippo Sisters
try for the record
at the roundabout,'
suggested Croc.

'No!' said Fox.
**'I came here
to score a goal
and I'm not
leaving till
I do.'**

Fox realised he was still wearing the golden
boots from the second–hand shop.
'Maybe these boots could help.'
'Good idea, Foxy,'
said Wombat.
He and Croc
sat down under
a palm tree
to watch.

Fox ran in and kicked the ball as hard as he had ever kicked a ball before.

It flew low,

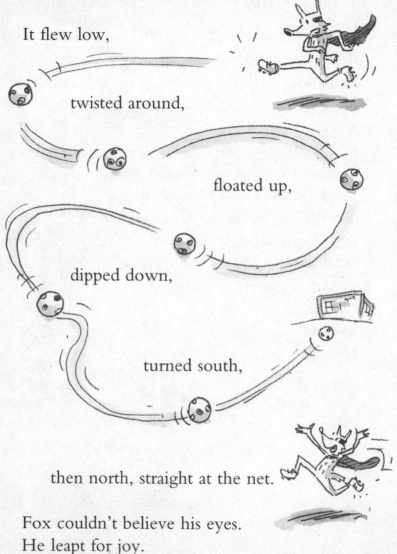

    twisted around,

                floated up,

        dipped down,

                turned south,

        then north, straight at the net.

Fox couldn't believe his eyes.
He leapt for joy.

Alas, too soon!

At the last moment the
ball turned west and
flew wide of the goal.

Fox slumped to the ground.

'NNNNNOOOOOOOOO!!'

he cried.
'My 126th
miss in
a row!'

Fox tried to calm himself.
'These are *golden* boots,' he said.
'With these I cannot miss.'
Fox tried again.

And again.

And again.

'I must be rushing it,' said Fox.
On attempt number 134,
he took it very slowly.

He re-tied his wonderful
golden boots.

He straightened
his cape.

He adjusted
his tail.

Then he lined up the goal.
Fox ran in and kicked the ball.

This was
the worst kick of all.

The ball flew
straight up in the air.
Very high!

It hovered for a moment,
then fell back down.

It bounced off
Fox's head.

This was all too much.

At last Fox did what I would
have done ages ago.

He gave up!

'I'VE HAD ENOUGH OF
TRYING TO KICK GOALS
WITH MY CROOKED FEET!'
he shouted.

'AND I'VE HAD
ENOUGH OF
THESE STUPID
GOLDEN
BOOTS!'

With all his strength, Fox threw
his golden boots into a tree.

It was the
very same tree
where the bird family
was settling down to sleep
for the night in their new letterbox nest.
Fox's golden boots crashed into the
letterbox nest and knocked
it out of the tree.
And the poor birds were
made homeless for
the second time
that day.

'AND I'VE HAD ENOUGH OF THIS STUPID SOCCER BALL!'

Fox booted the ball into the lake.

Only he missed the lake.

The ball curved.

To his left.

Your right.

It flew into the GOAL!!!

'What?' said Fox.
'I don't believe it! I kicked a goal!'

And just to be sure it wasn't a fluke, he
retrieved the ball and kicked it towards
the lake again.

And again the ball curved
around and flew into the goal.

This was no fluke.

Fox danced.

And whooped.

And hollered.

And did handstands.

Fox ran over to the palm tree.
'DID YOU SEE THAT,
WOMBAT?' he cried.
'I SCORED
A GOAL!'

But Wombat wasn't there.
Nor was Croc.

Instead, there was a note pinned to the
palm tree.

'Foxy,
Croc and I have gone
to watch the Hippo
Sisters riding around
the roundabout.
Good luck!'

Fox couldn't believe it.
He had finally kicked a goal
and Wombat wasn't there to see it.

Fox was angry.
But he was also happy.

He was more happy than angry.
After all, he had kicked a goal.

Two goals!

'Just call me Superfox Goldenboot,' he said.

That night Fox slept soundly.
After 134 misses in a row, even though
nobody actually saw him do it,
FOX HAD FINALLY KICKED A GOAL!

TWO GOALS!

And you might like to know that the birds
in the tree slept soundly, too.
Fox's golden boots made a very fine nest.

Two very fine nests.

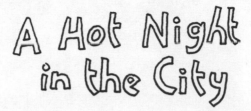

A Hot Night in the City

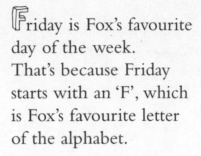

Friday is Fox's favourite day of the week. That's because Friday starts with an 'F', which is Fox's favourite letter of the alphabet.

This Friday was very hot. The temperature gauge on the Oldmeadow building hovered around 40 degrees.

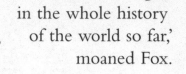

'This is the hottest night
in the whole history
of the world so far,'
moaned Fox.

Beads of sweat
appeared on
his forehead…

…rolled down
the furrows
of his brow…

…ran down
his long nose
and pooled
behind the black
bit at the end…

…then dripped
onto the carpet.

'Let's go
to Gorilla's place,'
said Wombat.
**'She has an
airconditioner.'**

'No,' said Fox.
'The Five Monkeys
will be there!'

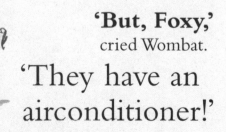

'So,'
said Wombat.

'They are annoying!'
said Fox.
'I'm staying here.'

'But, Foxy,'
cried Wombat.
'They have an
airconditioner!'

Fox refused to budge,
so they stayed in
Fox's apartment
and
sweltered.

After dinner, Fox decided
to go to bed early.
'G'night, Wombat!'
'G'night, Fox!'

Fox lay
on his bed
trying to sleep.

But he
couldn't.

His pillow
was too flat.

Then too hot.

'How can I sleep with a too-hot,
too-flat pillow!'

Soon the bedbugs
began to bite as well.

Then mosquitoes arrived
and buzzed around
Fox's head, waiting
for an opening –
which they
eventually found.

'OUCH!

Stupid mosquitoes!'

Fox swiped and
slapped at them.
He tried to squash
them on the wall
with his pillow.
All he succeeded
in doing was falling
off his bed, bumping
into his bedside chest
and knocking over
his glass of water.

'Must have water!'

gasped Fox.

He staggered to the fridge, but the water jug was empty. There was no ice either. The water in the kitchen tap was warm.

So Fox staggered to the bathroom. The water is always cooler in there.

'ARGH!'

cried Fox.

'There's a RAT
IN THE BATH!
A HUGE HAIRY RAT!'

Fox
ran about
the bathroom
screaming,
**'RAT!
RAT!
RAT!'**

So Wombat joined in.
'Rat! Rat! Rat!'
they both yelled.

Fox stopped.
'Is that you, Wombat?
I thought you were a big fat rat!
What are you doing in my bath?'

'I was hot,' said Wombat.
'So I took all the ice and cold
water out of the fridge and tipped
it into the bath. And I got in and
I must have fallen asleep.'
Wombat and Fox sat
together in the bath,
till all the ice melted.
The temperature
reached 42 degrees.

'Gorilla's got airconditioning,'
suggested Wombat.
'No,' said Fox.
'Okay, I've got a better idea, Foxy.
Let's go for a swim.'
'Where?' asked Fox.
'In the fountain outside.'

A few minutes later, Wombat and Fox rushed
out of their building and on to the street.

'Last one in is a rotten tomato,'
yelled Wombat.

His fat little
wombat legs
were never going to
be faster than those of his
longer, leaner foxy friend.

Fox sprinted past Wombat and
took a flying leap into the fountain.
'NOOOooo!' he yelled.
'The fountain's empty!'

Fox landed with a sickening crash.
A puff of dust wafted up from the
dry fountain.
It had been a long hot summer,
with water restrictions.
All the city's fountains
were dry.

'Are you okay, Foxy?'
asked Wombat.
Fox's head appeared.
'You're a rotten tomato!' he said,
then collapsed back into the fountain.

'Last one in is a pig's bottom!'
called a familiar voice.
It was Croc,
running down the hill.

'Stop, Croc!'
Wombat yelled.
**'There's
no water!'**

Too late!

Croc leapt into
the fountain.

There was a loud hollow thud – like the sound of a crocodile landing on a fox who is lying on concrete.

And a puff of dust.

The thud caused plates to rattle in nearby apartments.

Babies woke from their slumbers.

Whole buildings trembled.

And Fox's ribs almost broke.

Wombat, Fox and Croc
sat quietly on the edge of the fountain.
The temperature gauge on the Oldmeadow
building glowed 45 degrees.

'Sooo hot,' gasped Fox.
'Let's go swim in Gorilla's
pool,' said Wombat.
Fox massaged his aching ribs.
'I want to go home
and sit in the dark.'

Anything was better
than facing the
Five Monkeys.

'I'm so hot
I could eat
the top off a
fire hydrant,'
announced Croc.

'Now, that gives me an idea,' said Wombat.
He pointed to the fire hydrant
across the street.
'Are you thinking
what I'm thinking?'
'Not likely,' said Croc.
'It's Friday. I don't
think on Fridays.'

Wombat crossed the road to the hydrant.
He climbed on top and tried
to turn it on.
But it wouldn't budge.
'It needs a special
handle,' he said.

'Stand aside,' announced Fox.
'This is a job for **Superfox**
with jaws of steel.'
Fox grasped the top
of the hydrant
in his teeth.

'This is never
going to work,'
said Wombat.
'But it's fun to watch,'
said Croc.

Fox struggled with the hydrant until finally a few of his teeth fell out and dropped onto the footpath.

'My beautiful teeth!'
he cried.

'Let me try,' said Croc. She pulled on the fire hydrant. Eventually the heavy cast-iron top broke off and flew high up into the air, on a powerful jet of water.

Fox went up
with it.

Then Fox plummeted
back to earth.
'I'll catch you,'
cried Croc.

But at the last
moment Croc slipped
and fell in the pool
of water around
the hydrant.

Fox crashed to the
ground and the heavy
cast-iron top of the
fire hydrant
crashed down
on his head.
It knocked
him out cold.

Wombat splashed water
on Fox's face.
Croc tapped him
lightly on the cheek.
'You have to give him
mouth-to-mouth,'
said Wombat.
**'Mouth-
to-mouth?'**
cried Croc.
'Why me?'

Fox's eyes flickered open.
'Hrrmmaa pphhaar brrr!'
he groaned.
'Are you all right, Foxy?'
asked Wombat.
Fox blinked.
He could see two Wombats.
He blinked again.
Now there were four.

A crowd had gathered, splashing about
in the large pool around the hydrant.
The Five Monkeys were there, too.
They were playing under the waterfall
and not making room for anyone else.

Then the Hippo Sisters rode up on their
bicycle, which had a new flashing light
and a new siren. And a trailer.
They were wearing Water Board uniforms.
They pushed all the people
back and put up barriers
around the hydrant.
The Five Monkeys
complained.

'**Go back inside
your houses,**'
the Hippo Sisters yelled.
'**There's nothing
to see here.**'

Wombat, Fox and Croc moved to the bench
outside the supermarket. The temperature
gauge on the Oldmeadow building had
reached 46 degrees.

'I'm so hot,' said Fox. 'I wish I was a penguin.'
'I wish I was a frozen chicken,' said Croc.
'Clever Croc,' said Wombat.
'That gives me an idea.'

Wombat led his friends into the supermarket.
In the frozen-food aisle,
he pulled back the sliding door.
'We can lie a
while in here,'
he said, stepping into the
frozen-food
freezer.

'Not so fast, fat Wombat,' said a voice.
'The Five Monkeys!' cried Fox.
'What are you doing here?'

'The same as you,' said the middle monkey.
'Stupid Hippo Sisters turned the water off,'
said the second-youngest monkey.
'I was so hot, I nearly fainted,' said the
youngest monkey. 'So we came here.'

'Shove over and let us in,' said Fox.
'Buzz off!' shouted the Five Monkeys,
throwing frozen peas at Wombat,
Fox and Croc.
And they slammed the freezer door closed.

Wombat, Fox and Croc left the supermarket
and walked down Celestial Avenue.
It was now 47 degrees.
'I'm so hot,' said Fox,
'I could eat an iceberg.'
'I could eat
a polar bear,'
said Croc.

'Very clever, Croc,' said Wombat.
'That gives me another idea.
Let's go to the Penguin Brothers Ice Factory.
They throw all the broken iceblocks out
into the backyard.'
'This will be so cool,' said Fox.

They snuck around to the backyard, quietly,
so they didn't wake the Penguin Brothers.
But guess what!

They were too late.
There were five blocks of ice with a monkey
bottom sitting on each one.

'Not fair,' cried Fox.

'Too slow,' said the oldest monkey.
'They threw us out of the supermarket,'
  said the second-oldest monkey.
'So we came straight here,'
  said the middle monkey.
'We took the short cut,'
  said the second-youngest monkey.
'We hurried so fast, I nearly fainted,'
  said the youngest monkey.

Wombat, Fox and Croc walked along the
river bank, past the supermarket car park.

'Hello,' called a voice.
'Hi, Gorilla,' said Wombat.
'It sure is a hot night,
Wombat,' said Gorilla.
'Why don't you pop
around to our place
for a swim in our pool?
The Five Monkeys
would love to see you.
They haven't been
out for three days
and they are
getting restless.'

'What do you mean they haven't been
out for three days?' asked Wombat.
'They were very naughty,' said Gorilla.
'I won't go into details,
but they are grounded
for a week.'
'Is that so?'
said Wombat.

'Airconditioning, a pool and NO
Five Monkeys!' whispered Fox.
'What are we waiting for?'
Wombat, Fox and
Croc went home
with Gorilla.

She made
banana pancakes,
banana muffins
and banana
milkshakes.

With extra banana.

'I hate banana,'
said Fox.
'Can I have
yours?' asked Croc.
'I love banana.'

'Are the Five Monkeys going to have some?'
asked Wombat.
'Poor darlings,' said Gorilla. 'They are
in their room, watching TV.'

'Let's go for a swim,'
said Fox.
'Great thinking, Foxy,'
said Wombat.
'The water looks so cool.'

'Last one in is a rotten tomato!' cried Croc,
and she leapt into the pool.

At that moment
the Five Monkeys
tumbled over
the back gate.

They all pointed at Fox.
'What are you doing at our house, skinny
chest?' asked the oldest monkey.
'Stupid cape,' said the second-oldest monkey.
'Weird mask,' said the middle monkey.
And they all laughed at Fox.

'So, my monkey friends,'
said Wombat.
'Gorilla told us you
weren't allowed
out of the house.'
He fixed them
with his special
Wombat stare.

The
Five Monkeys
fell silent.
Then the oldest
monkey said,
'You won't tell her, will you?
She'll skin us alive if she finds out.'
'Of course I won't tell,' said Wombat.
'Unless I forget.'

'Unless you forget what?'

cried the second-oldest monkey.
'Unless I forget to remember,' said Wombat.
'Now we are going for a swim and we don't
wish to be disturbed.'
'Anything you say,
Wombat,' chorused
the Five Monkeys.

Wombat gave them one last special stare,
then he joined Croc in the pool.

Fox stood watching
the Five Monkeys.
They said nothing.
No sniggers.
No pointing.
No pinching.
No nasty remarks.

'Bring us some icy cold drinks,' said Fox.
He closed one eye and opened the other one
wide, trying to copy the
special Wombat stare.

'Right away, Fox,'
the Five Monkeys
said, hurrying
to the door.

'With lots of ice!' Fox added,

giving them that Wombat stare again.

'Or I'll tell Gorilla.'

The monkeys hurried down the hall, tripping
over each other as they went.

Then Fox smiled
a broad smile
and dived
into the pool.

WOMBAT & FOX

BOOK 2

SUMMER in the CITY

I Spy

'I'm melting!' said Fox.
'I'm melting more,' said Wombat.
'This is the hottest summer ever,' said Fox.
'My fur is falling out in clumps.'
'We've got to get out of the city, Foxy.'

The next morning, Wombat bounded
into Fox's kitchen.
'Foxy! I've fixed it. We're going on a seaside
holiday. Bandicoot has loaned us his beach
box for a week.'

'Foxy?'
Wombat looked around the room.
'Foxy! Where are you?'

Wombat peeped inside Fox's room.
His friend was fast asleep.

Wombat picked up Fox's trumpet,
and blew as hard as
he could.

'**Pppaaaarrpp!!!**'

'Wake up, Foxy.
We're going on a
summer holiday!'

Fox hit the roof.
'Fire!

Fire!'

he yelled.

He bounced
around the
room looking
for a way out.
He rushed
through a door.

Wrong door.

'Come out of the cupboard, Foxy,' said Wombat.
'It's time to go.'

'But I have to pack,' said Fox.
'No time to chat, Foxy! Quickly or we'll
miss the early bus and waste the first day
of our holiday.'
Fox grabbed his suitcase and they scrambled
out the door.

Halfway down the road, Fox cried,
'I forgot to pack my toothbrush!'
'You can share mine,' said Wombat.
'Yeeecchh!' said Fox. 'No way.'

Wombat and Fox arrived at the bus stop
just as a bus was pulling away.
'We're too late,' said Wombat.
'I hope there's another bus.'

They waited. And waited.
Eventually another bus
appeared at the top of the hill.
'Is that our bus?' asked Fox.
'No,' said Wombat. 'Our bus will have
a *To the beach* sign on it.'

So they waited.
The next bus didn't have a *To the beach*
sign on it either.

Nor the next one.
Nor the one after that.

Finally Wombat hailed a bus.
'Does this bus go to the beach?' he asked
the driver.
'All these buses go to the beach,'
said the driver.
'Oh,' said Wombat.

Wombat and Fox scrambled onto the bus.
As they walked up the aisle, Fox tripped over
a foot.

Five feet.

It was the Five Monkeys.

They laughed and pointed at Fox.
'What are you doing on our bus?'
asked Wombat.
'We're going to the beach for a holiday.'
'Oh, no,' said Fox. 'This could be
the worst holiday of my life!'
'We hope so,' said the oldest monkey and
they all laughed at Fox.
Then, the second-oldest
monkey stuck his
chewing gum in the
lock on Fox's suitcase.

Wombat and Fox found a seat up the back
away from the Five Monkeys.
Fox tried to open his suitcase, but the lock
was gummed up.

'Oh, no,' he said. 'I can't open my
suitcase. And I think I left my
sunglasses at home.'

'I spy the sea,' said Wombat.
'No way,' said Fox. 'And that's not how you
 play I-Spy.'
'But I can see the sea,' said Wombat.
'Between those buildings – a small bit of blue.'

'That's not the sea,' said Fox.
'Yes it is.'
'No, it isn't.'

Fox fiddled with his gummed-up lock.
'I spy the sea again,' said Wombat.

The bus stopped for a passenger.
'Hello,' said a familiar voice.

'Croc!' said Fox.
'What are you doing on our bus?'
'I'm going to the beach for a summer
holiday,' she said.
'So are we,' said Wombat. 'Sit with us.'

So they all squeezed
together onto the
one seat.

'Let's play I-Spy,' said Croc.
'You start, Croc,' said Fox.
'I spy with my little eye
a *bus*,' said Croc.

'That's not how it works,' said Fox.
'You have to give a letter not a thing.'
'Oh,' said Croc. 'That's much harder.'

Croc looked up and down and all around.
She tried again. 'I spy with my little eye
something beginning with *C*.'
'Cat,' said Fox leaping out of his seat.
'Nup!' said Croc.

'Car,' said Fox.
'Nup!'

'Clock,' cried Fox.
'Nup,' said Croc.

Fox kept guessing for longer than anyone
else in the universe would have bothered.
'Do you give up?'
asked Croc. 'It's a *bus*!'

'**A bus?** *Bus* doesn't start with **C**!'
cried Fox. 'You have to say the letter the
thing starts with ... not just *any* letter!'
'Golly,' said Croc. 'It's a much harder game
than I thought.'

'Let me show you how it works. I spy with
my little eye something beginning with **K**,'
said Fox.
'Rubbish bin!' said Croc.
'No!' Fox shouted.
'*Rubbish bin*
doesn't start
with **K**!'

'Bus conductors!' said Croc.

'**NNNOOO!**' screamed Fox.

'Bus conductors doesn't start with **K**, either!!'

'No,' said Croc. 'I mean bus conductors on the bus!'

'Excuse us,' said the two bus conductors. 'Can we see your tickets?'

'Hippo Sisters!' said Wombat. 'I didn't know
you had new jobs. Great uniforms!'
'Tickets please,' said the bigger of the
two Hippo Sisters.
'We don't have any tickets,' said Wombat.
'No tickets?' said the other Hippo Sister.
'Nobody told us we needed tickets!'
said Wombat.

'I have a ticket,' said Croc.
She showed it to the Hippo Sisters.
'Well done, Croc,' said the Hippo Sisters.
'You can stay on the bus, but your friends
will have to get off.'

The bus stopped and the Hippo Sisters escorted Wombat and Fox off the bus. The Five Monkeys pushed past the Hippo Sisters and scrambled off, too. They didn't have tickets either. Nor did the twenty Little Penguins.

Wombat and Fox
and the Five Monkeys
and the twenty Little Penguins
huddled on the footpath
as the bus drove off.

'Where are we, Wombat?' asked Fox.
'Don't know, Foxy.'
'How do we get to the beach?'
'Not sure, Foxy.'
'This is a disaster!' said Fox. 'We won't
get there till dark. And I can't get into
my suitcase, and I think I left my
sleeping bag at home.'
'Have you got *anything* in that suitcase
of yours, Foxy?'

'Ha! Ha!' said the oldest monkey. 'We know
you are staying at Bandicoot's beach box.'
'And we know the way there,' said the
second-oldest monkey.
'And we're not telling you,' said the middle
monkey.
'And we're going to get there first,' said the
second-youngest monkey.
'And you'll have to sleep up a tree,' said the
youngest monkey.

The Five Monkeys ran across the road and disappeared down a laneway so quickly that Wombat and Fox couldn't follow them.

'The Little Penguins will know where the beach is,' said Fox. 'Let's follow them.'

But the Little Penguins had just accepted a lift from a bus full of tourists.

'Someone must know the way,' said Fox.
An old lady walked towards them.
'Excuse me, old lady. Do you know how to get to the beach?' asked Fox.
'Yes, of course I do,'
said the old lady.
And she kept walking.
Fox scratched his
head and looked
at Wombat.

'We could ring Bandicoot and ask him,'
Wombat suggested. 'Do you have your
phone, Foxy?'

'Why do we always end up using
MY phone?' Fox grumbled.

'Mine's out of credit,' said Wombat.

Fox tried to open his suitcase.

'Stupid monkeys,' he cried.
'It's still stuck with chewing gum!
And anyway,
I think I
forgot to pack
my phone!'

'This is a disaster, Wombat. No phone.
No sleeping bag. No toothbrush.
No ticket. And now the Five Monkeys are
going to kick us out of our holiday house.
This could be my worst holiday ever!'

Wombat and Fox sat together for a while.
Time out for a good long think never does
anyone any harm.

'The beach can't be far,' said Wombat.
'I could see the sea from the bus.'
'No you couldn't,' said Fox.

'I can smell hamburgers,' said Wombat.
'Forget food!' cried Fox. 'We have to beat the
Five Monkeys to Bandicoot's beach box.'

'Remember how last time we came to the
beach we bought the best hamburgers ever?'
'No!'
'How could you forget them, Foxy?'
Wombat sniffed the air.
'I think I remember where the shop was.
Follow me.'

'This is no time to be thinking of your stomach, Wombat!'
'Foxy, this is exactly the time to
TRUST THE STOMACH.'

They crossed the road and turned a corner
and a few minutes later they were outside
the hamburger shop. Wombat licked his lips.

'Do you remember what we ate after the hamburgers, Foxy?'
'I don't even remember the hamburgers!'
'After the best hamburger ever, I was still hungry so we found a cake shop.'
'So?' cried Fox.
'Which way stomach?' Wombat whispered to his rumbling belly.

They walked through a shopping mall, crossed a small playground and through a car park.
'I spy something starting with **C**!' said Wombat.
'Cake shop!' cried Fox.

'TRUST THE STOMACH, Foxy.
It never forgets.'
Wombat looked in the window of the most
magnificent cake shop in the universe.
His eyes welled with tears.
'Are you sure you don't have any money in
that suitcase, Foxy?'
'I can't even *open* the suitcase!' said Fox.

'Never mind,' said Wombat. 'We have no time
for cakes if we are going to beat the Five
Monkeys to our beach box.'
'Which way now?' asked Fox.
Wombat raised his nose and took
a deep breath.
'Ice-cream,' he said, and his stomach gave
a loud gurgle. 'We'll take the short cut.'

They hurried down an alley, climbed a ladder
and soon found themselves high up on the roof
of a church with a view of the whole suburb.

'There it is!' announced Wombat.
'The ice-cream cart. **And the beach**!'
'And there are the Five Monkeys,'
cried Fox. 'On the boardwalk!'

Wombat and Fox
ran down the stairs as fast
as their feet would carry them.
Until Fox's clumsy legs got
tangled up with his suitcase.

They slid down the
rest of the stairs and
tumbled out the door
at the bottom.

'The Five Monkeys are going to beat us,'
cried Fox.
'Oh, no they won't,' said Wombat.
He bundled Fox and his suitcase into
a shopping trolley.

At ground level all the streets looked the same.
'I'm not sure which road to take,' said Wombat.
Fox looked him in the eye and said,
'TRUST THE STOMACH, Wombat!'

Wombat smiled
and sniffed the wind.
He picked up a faint scent.
Sea air.

Getting stronger.
Sea air and suncream.

Even stronger.
Sea air, suncream, fish and chips
and a faint whiff of ice-cream.
'This way,' said Wombat, pushing
the trolley down the hill.

They rolled towards the beach,
picking up speed.

Soon Wombat wasn't
pushing the trolley.
The trolley was pulling Wombat.

'Uh, oh!' cried Wombat.
'NNNOOO!!' cried Fox.

They flashed down the hill.
'Do something!' screamed Fox.

Wombat did something.
He hopped onboard.
And the two friends rode
the trolley down the hill...

SMASH!

and crashed into the Five Monkeys!
Wombat and Fox and Fox's suitcase and
the Five Monkeys all bounced off the
boardwalk and into the sea.

A passing boat fished them out and
returned them to the pier.
'Are you all right, Foxy?' called Wombat.

'No!' cried Fox. 'I am wet through.
My suitcase is full of water and
the Five Monkeys
are going to beat
us to Bandicoot's
beach box.'

Hee.
Hee.

'At least you can see the sea now,'
said Wombat.

'Humppphhh!!' grunted Fox.

Wombat helped Fox to his feet, picked up his
suitcase and they ran up the steps.

'The Five Monkeys are too fast,' said Fox.
'They will take over Bandicoot's beach box.
This *is* a disaster!'

Suddenly the Five Monkeys ran down the stairs. They were screaming and whimpering as they ran right past Wombat and Fox.

'I wonder what happened?' said Wombat.

When Wombat and Fox finally arrived at
the beach box they were greeted by Croc.
'It's about time you got here,' she said.
'The Five Monkeys decided to leave in a hurry.'
She held up a piece of one of their tails.

Fox dragged his suitcase inside.
The sea water had hardened
the chewing gum and
he was able to pry
it out of the lock.
Inside Fox found
his toothbrush and
his phone and his
sunglasses, sleeping bag,
sunscreen and pillow.

'I did pack everything,' said Fox.

Wombat and Fox put all their wet things
out to dry on the roof of the beach box.

'Let's sit on the sand, Foxy,' said Wombat.
'There's still a few hours of the afternoon left.
The sun will warm us up.'

So Wombat, Fox and Croc
made themselves comfortable.
Then it started to rain.

And The Winner Is...

On the Sunday of Wombat and Fox's
beach holiday it rained all day.
It rained on Monday too.
And Tuesday.
And Wednesday as well.

By Thursday morning Wombat and Fox and
Croc were getting a little crazy cooped up in
Bandicoot's tiny beach box.
Fox was sick of Croc.
And Croc was sick of Fox.

And everyone was sick of Wombat's
baked beans, which were all they
had eaten for five days.
Cold baked beans.

click!

Wombat peeked out the door
of the beach box.
'Guess what?' he announced.
'The rain has stopped.'
Fox and Croc rushed outside.
Sure enough the sun
was shining.

Click!

'I bags the hammock,' said Fox. He dived into
it and opened his *Caped Corgi* comic.
'But it's my turn,' said Croc.
'No,' said Fox. 'It was
your turn yesterday.'

'But it was raining
yesterday,'
said Croc.

Smile!

'Come with me,'
said Wombat, dragging
Croc away from Fox and the hammock.

They walked along the beach and found
the perfect spot to lie in the sun.

'I'm so hot,' Croc complained.
'Go for a swim' said Wombat.
'It's too crowded,' said Croc. 'I like to be able
to bodysurf without crashing into people.'

'I know how to cool you down,' said Wombat,
'I'll bury you in the sand.'
'But I'll drown?'
'You can't drown in sand, Croc,' said Wombat.
'Here, these will help.'
Wombat stuck two straws up Croc's nostrils.
'Now you can breathe under the sand,' said
Wombat. 'And I'll put my towel over your
head, so you won't get sand in your eyes.'

Wombat set about covering Croc's body
with sand. She was a big Croc so it took
a long time.

Finally Wombat stood back and admired
his work. 'That will keep you nice and cool,'
he said.

After all that work,
Wombat was very tired,
so he lay with his head
on the lump that was Croc
and soon they were both fast asleep.

Back at the beach box, Fox was on to his
second comic.

A mosquito buzzed around his head.

Then a dragonfly flew by.

Then a bright green beetle.

The beetle was out of control and
bumped into the beach box,
then the tree, then
Fox's comic and finally…

it flew up Fox's nose.

Fox coughed
and spluttered
and lost his balance entirely,
which is a bad thing to do in a hammock.
Fox spun around and around until he was
so tightly wound up in his hammock that
he couldn't move.
Then he sneezed and the bright green beetle
flew out of his nose.

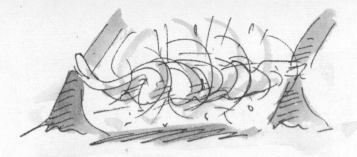

The twisted-up hammock untwisted.
It untwisted with such force that it flipped
Fox up into the air and down onto the sand.

'Stupid hammock!' he yelled.

And he ran off along the beach.

'Wombat!'

'Wombat!'

'What's the problem, Foxy?'

'It's a medical emergency!' said Fox.

'I had a green beetle up my nose.'

'Sounds serious,' said Wombat.

'It *is* serious,' cried Fox.

'I might have beetle-nose!'

'Let me look, Foxy,' said Wombat.
'You're not touching my nose.
I need a proper nurse to do that.'
'Okay,' said Wombat. 'There's a first-aid tent
at the other end of the beach.'

As Wombat and Fox hurried along the beach,
they passed the twenty Little Penguins who
were busy building a sand sculpture.
All the penguins were working as a team,
bucketing and spading and wetting and
smoothing the sand.
And singing as they worked.

'Wow,' said Wombat. 'That's a work of art.'
'Thank you,' said Big Penguin.

'What is it?' asked Fox.
'It's a fish,' said Big Penguin. 'It's an Atlantic
Salmon. South Atlantic, that is. Not the
common North Atlantic Salmon.'

'Oh,' said Wombat.
He had no idea what a South Atlantic
Salmon looked like.
Neither did Fox.

Trust me, it was a VERY good likeness
of a South Atlantic Salmon.
Those penguins sure knew their fish.

'You should join the competition,' said Big
Penguin. 'The winner gets ten dollars.'
'And a blue ribbon,' said Penguin Seven.
'And a tube of lip balm,' said Penguin Thirteen.

'What competition?' asked Wombat.
'The Summer Sand Sculpture Competition,' said
Big Penguin. 'You've gotta be in it to win it.'

'That's a great idea,' said Fox.
'Let's do it.'

'Wombat, if we win the ten dollars we wouldn't have to eat baked beans anymore,' said Fox. 'We could eat like kings for the rest of our holiday.'

Wombat and Fox walked straight past the first-aid tent to the Official Summer Sand Sculpture Competition tent.

'Stay here, Wombat,' said Fox. 'I'll sort this out.'

A few minutes later Fox skipped out of the tent with two buckets and two spades. 'We're in!' he said. 'And they gave us these for free.'

Wombat and Fox rushed back along the
beach looking for the best spot to build
their sand sculpture.

They saw Water Rat by the edge of the sea.
He was building a drip-castle.
He had handfuls of very wet sand that he let
drip through his fingers to slowly build
up sturdy walls and tall towers.
'Hi, Water Rat,' said Wombat.
'That's a clever idea.
Do you mind
if we try it too?'
'It takes a special
talent,' said Water Rat.
'You have to *understand*
the water.'

Wombat and Fox soon discovered that building
a drip-castle was much harder than it looked.
Their walls and towers kept collapsing.
Fox tried to stay calm.
'Be patient, Foxy,' said Wombat.

'I can't work with this stupid wet sand!'
wailed Fox.

'Okay. Let's try where the sand is drier,'
said Wombat.

They found a spot where there were already
some small sand hills.

'We can use these as the foundation for our
sand sculpture,' said Wombat.
'We can build a Grand Summer Palace!'

They collected buckets full of damp sand
to add to the hill. They piled and patted
and carved and smoothed and shaped
it into a sand sculpture.

The Grand Summer Palace was magnificent,
but a bit wobbly.
It had rounded walls and fancy windows,
curved domes and many tall towers and a
moat with a big bridge. And it was decorated
with seaweed flags and plastic lolly wrappers.

The Little Penguins gathered around
to admire it.
'It is wonderful,' said Big Penguin.
'You'll win for sure.'
'I think we might,' said Fox.

The Five Monkeys suddenly appeared.
'Ha! Ha! It looks like a sleeping dinosaur,'
said the oldest monkey.
'A dead sleeping dinosaur,' said the youngest
monkey.
'Ours is better!' said the middle monkey.
'Ours will win for sure,' said the oldest
monkey.
'No, it won't,' said Fox. 'Ours will
definitely win.'

'I bet you my bed it won't,'
said the second-oldest monkey.
'I bet you my bed *and*
my pillow it will,' said Fox.

'I bet you all our food it won't,'
said the middle monkey.

'I bet you our beach box it will,'
said Fox

'Deal!' said the middle monkey.

'Deal!' said Fox.

'Did you make a bet with the Five Monkeys,
Foxy?' asked Wombat.
'Yes. I bet we would win the competition.'
'Oh,' said Wombat.

'Don't worry, Wombat. We will win the
competition AND we will win the Five
Monkeys' food as well. This is going to be
the best holiday ever.'
'What if we lose?' asked Wombat.
'Think positive, Wombat!' said Fox.
'There is no way we will lose!'

'Have you seen the Five Monkeys' entry,
Foxy? It's very good.'
The Five Monkeys' sand sculpture
wasn't just good.
It was brilliant.
And huge.
A dazzling construction of sand and
shells in the shape of an attacking shark.

It was so lifelike that Penguin Seventeen
and Eighteen ran away and hid.

'PPPfffffaaaafff!'

A little hooter sounded.
'That's it,' said the Hippo Sisters. 'Time's up.'

They marched along the beach telling
everyone to stop building.

'Hello, Wombat,' said the bigger of the two
Hippo Sisters. 'Don't count on winning just
because my sister thinks you're cute.'
The smaller Hippo Sister blushed.
Then she giggled.

The judges looked at each entry.
They loved Water Rat's drip-castle.
It was spectacular.

They were very impressed with the twenty
Little Penguins' South Atlantic Salmon.

They stood in front of Wombat and Fox's
Grand Summer Palace and made many notes.
But they kept their distance from the
Five Monkeys' Attack Shark.

The judges returned to Water Rat's drip-castle.
The bigger of the two Hippo Sisters
stepped forward.
'Ladies and gentlemen,' she said.
'We are pleased to announce the winner
of the Summer Sand Sculpture Competition.
The first prize goes to—'

Suddenly a big wave from a passing boat
crashed onto the beach.

It swamped Water Rat's drip-castle and
turned it into a pile of dribbly sand hills.
A second wave washed it away altogether.

Water Rat sniffed,
and shrugged his shoulders.
'Oh, well,' he said. 'The water
gives and the water takes away.'

The Hippo Sisters
moved on.

'Listen up, everyone!' said the bigger
of the two sisters. 'The new winners are the
Five Monkeys for their Attack Shark.'

The Five Monkeys danced around Fox.
'Ha! Ha! Fox! We are the winners!'
sang the oldest monkey.
'NNNOOOOO!' cried Fox.

'You are the loser!' sang the second-oldest monkey pointing at Fox.

'NNNOOOOO!!' cried Fox.

'We get your beach box, said the middle monkey.

'FOXY?' cried Wombat.

'You bet Bandicoot's beach box!'

'We built the best sculpture,'
sang the second-youngest monkey.
'And I blew it up all by myself,'
sang the youngest monkey.

'Shush!' said the other four monkeys.

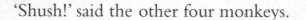

'Blew it up?'
said Wombat and Fox together.

'Can I take a photo of you pinning the ribbon on the winning sculpture?' Wombat called to the judges.

The Hippo Sisters smiled big smiles as they pinned the blue ribbon to the Attack Shark. The Five Monkeys tried to stop her.

But it was too late.

There was a pop and a loud hissing noise.
And slowly the Five Monkeys'
Attack Shark collapsed.

The judges kicked at the sand and found the
Five Monkeys had built their sculpture over
the youngest monkey's plastic inflatable shark.

'The Five Monkeys are
disqualified for cheating!'
announced the judges.

'We award the prize to Wombat and Fox
for their Grand Summer Palace. It is a bit
wonky, but at least it stands up.'

'I am the winner!' sang Fox.
'The Five Monkeys have
to give me all their food.'
He did a little winner's dance around
the Little Penguins and the Five Monkeys.
'I am the winner and
you are the losers!' he sang.

The Hippo Sisters stepped forward to pin the
blue ribbon on Fox's winning sand sculpture.
'Please,' said Fox. 'Can I do that?'
'Certainly,' said the Hippo sisters.
'Take a photo of me winning, Wombat.'

Fox tried to pin the ribbon on the
Grand Summer Palace.
But the ribbon wouldn't stick.

So Fox pushed harder.
It still wouldn't stick.
'Stupid ribbon!'

Fox pushed the pin in
with all his might.
This time it stuck.

The Grand Summer
Palace began to wobble.

Then it shook violently.

Then it exploded!

'OOOWWW CCCHHHH!'

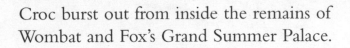

Croc burst out from inside the remains of Wombat and Fox's Grand Summer Palace.

'NNNOOOO!!'
cried Fox.

They had built their sand scultpure on a little
hill on the beach.
They didn't realise that the little hill was
Croc, still lying in the cool sand where
Wombat had buried her earlier that day.
Wombat stared sadly at the wreckage
of the Grand Summer Palace.

Meanwhile Fox was being chased along the
beach by an angry Croc.

So who did win the Summer Sand Sculpture
Competition?

The Little Penguins, of course!

The judges pinned the blue ribbon on their
South Atlantic Salmon and it didn't wash
away or deflate or explode.

They presented the Little Penguins
with their ten dollar prize.

And their blue ribbon.

And their tube
of lip balm.

What Crab Is That?

Whenever one of my holidays is coming to an end, I think of all the things I wish I had done but didn't get around to doing.
And so it was with Fox.

'We haven't been to Crab Island yet,' said Fox.
'I'm too busy doing nothing to do something,' said Wombat.
'No you're not,' said Fox. 'Today is the day.'

'Is Croc asleep?' asked Fox.
'She's snoring like a bulldozer,'
said Wombat.
'Okay, let's go,' said Fox.

Wombat and Fox ran along the
beach towards Crab Island.
'I feel bad that we snuck off on her, Foxy.'
'You'd feel worse if she came with us,'
said Fox. 'She'd scare away all the crabs.'

Wombat and Fox walked carefully across
the rock pools that led to Crab Island.
Fox turned over five rocks in a row.
'No crabs here,' he said.

'click!'

'Or here!'

'Or here!'

'Look, Foxy,' Wombat called.
'I found some squirts.'

Fox stared at the strange lumpy creatures
on the rocks.
'Why are they called squirts?' asked Fox,
poking at one.

A jet of sea water hit Fox in the face.

Fox chased Wombat across the rocky reef,
to the edge of a big, deep rock pool.

'Lots of sea creatures here,' said Wombat.
'Wow,' said Fox. 'A stripey starfish.'
'And a spotty one.'

'And an octopus!'
said Fox.

Fox poked it and
it stuck to his finger.

'Get off, stupid octopus!'

he cried, panicking and flicking his hand.

The octopus flew over Wombat's head
and landed in another
rock pool. It
quickly hid
in a crevice.

Fox found another rock
pool and dipped his hand into the water.
'There's a crab under this ledge, Wombat.'
He tried to pick it up.
The crab nipped Fox on the finger.

'Yeeeooww-
ccchhh!!'

he cried.

'There's a knack to handling crabs,' said
Wombat. 'Do you want me to show you?'

'No!' said Fox.

He looked at his
throbbing finger.

'Yes!'

'Grab them from behind, Foxy,'
said Wombat. 'So they can't nip you.'

Fox scooped one up from behind.
The crab tried to nip him, but its
claws were not long enough.
'Aha!' he said.
'That's easy.'

Fox wandered across Crab Island peering under rocks and into rock pools searching for crabs.

A few drops of water fell on his head.

Then a few more drops.

Then a whole lot of water splashed onto him.
Fox looked up.
There were no rain clouds.

Suddenly a wave
crashed over Fox.

Then another.

And another.

The Five Monkeys jumped up on top of the highest rock shelf. They were laughing and pointing and tossing buckets full of water onto Fox until he was drenched.

'Stop it!' yelled Fox.

'How did you get so wet?' asked Wombat.
'The Five Monkeys threw water on me,'
said Fox.
'I don't see any monkeys, Foxy?' said Wombat.

The Five Monkeys giggled from behind
a big rock.
Then they threw more buckets of water
until Wombat and Fox were both soaked.

'Okay,' said Fox.

'A water fight it is then!'

'Can't catch us,' called the second-oldest monkey as they all ran to hide behind the rocks at the far edge of the reef.

'Let's get them,' said Fox.
'No,' said Wombat.
'We don't need to.
Just wait.'

'Wait for what?' asked Fox.
Just then a set of large waves crashed over the
reef, completely drenching the Five Monkeys.
They squealed and ran away across the reef.

A little while later
Fox called to Wombat.
'Look, what I've
found. He held up
a whole bucketful
of crabs.'

'You are not meant to collect them,'
said a stern voice. It was Water Rat.
'You mustn't take crabs away from their
rock pools,' he said. 'That's not the way
of the water, young Fox.'
'It doesn't hurt them,' said Fox.
'The rock pool is their home,' said Water Rat.
'Put them back.'

'No way!' said Fox, standing defiantly
on the edge of the reef holding on to his
bucket of crabs.

At that moment another huge wave
crashed over the rocks and over Fox.

When the spray cleared, Fox was covered in crabs.

'OOOWWWCCCHH!!!'

he cried. 'Get off me, crazy crabs!'

Wombat brushed all the crabs off his friend. They scuttled back into hidey-holes under the rocks.

'Don't worry, Foxy,' said Wombat.
'I'll piggy-back you home and we can
patch you up.'

Wombat and Fox turned back towards
the rock bridge to the beach.
'Oh, no,' said Wombat.
'The tide's come in.
We're stranded!'

'Ha! Ha!' said the oldest monkey.
'You're stranded!'

'I don't know why you
 think it's so funny,'
 said Wombat.
'If we're stranded,
 then so are you.'

It took a moment for that to sink in.
'No!!!!!' screamed all Five
Monkeys at once. 'We're stranded!
We're gonna drown!'

The Five Monkeys ran around and around
in smaller and smaller circles as the tide
continued to come in and wash over the reef.

'We need help,' said Water Rat.
'It's too dangerous to swim, even for me.'

At that moment, a small boat floated by,
pushed by the wind.

'Look!' cried Wombat. 'It's Croc! She's
come to rescue us.'

Wombat and Fox jumped
up and down waving
and calling to Croc.
So did the Five Monkeys.
And Water Rat.

But Croc floated
right past them.

'She's still asleep,' said Wombat.
'Come on, Foxy, we'll have to swim for it.'

Wombat dived into the water and Fox
took a deep breath and followed.
So did the Five Monkeys.
And Water Rat.

Luckily, the tide pushed Croc back
towards them.
In fact, it pushed the boat right over them.

They all bobbed out from under it and
scuttled aboard, coughing and spluttering.

Croc opened her eyes.

'**Sharks!**' she cried.

Croc scrambled to her feet.

'**HELP!**' she screamed.

'Don't panic, Croc,'
said Wombat.
'It's just us.'

But it was too late. Croc had panicked.
The little boat tipped up and Croc, Wombat,
Fox, the Five Monkeys and Water Rat
all fell into the water.

The boat drifted away from them.

'Stay calm,' said Water Rat.
The water gives and the water takes away.'
A few seconds later, the tide brought the
boat back and Wombat, Fox, Croc,
the Five Monkeys and Water Rat
climbed back on board.

'Phew, that was lucky!' said Wombat.
'Now we can row back to shore.'
'No oars!' cried Fox.
'NNNNNOOOOO!!!!!'
cried the Five Monkeys.
The tide had taken
the oars away.

'**Help!**' cried Wombat.

'**Help!**' cried Fox.

'**Help!**' cried Croc.

'**Help!!!!!**'

cried the Five Monkeys.

'Quiet!' said Water Rat.
'There's something out there.'

Water Rat was right.
They could all hear a
strange chirping sound.

It came closer.
And soon it was all
around the little boat.
Suddenly Big Penguin shot out of the water
and landed on top of the youngest monkey.

'Hello,' he said. 'What are you fellows doing
out in the middle of the ocean?'
'Crabbing,' said Wombat.
'There are no crabs here,' said Big Penguin.
'Plenty of fish though,' said Penguin Eight.
'A feast of fish!' said eighteen other penguins,
their stomachs bulging.

'Could you swim us back in?' asked Wombat.
'Of course,' said Big Penguin.

So nineteen Little Penguins surrounded the
boat and pushed it back to the beach.

'We're having a huge fish fry up,'
said Big Penguin. 'Would you like to join
us? We have plenty of fish.'
'Hooray,' said Fox. 'I could eat an oversized
South Atlantic Salmon.'

As the sun set on their summer holiday
Wombat, Fox, Croc, the Five Monkeys and
Water Rat picnicked on the beach with their
penguin friends and ate their fill of fish.

Except Wombat, that is. He didn't eat any
of the Little Penguins' fish. It wasn't that
he didn't like fish. It was just
that he had seen how the
Little Penguins stored
their fish when they
were out at sea.

Wombat didn't have the
stomach for any fish.

Especially penguin-stomach fish!

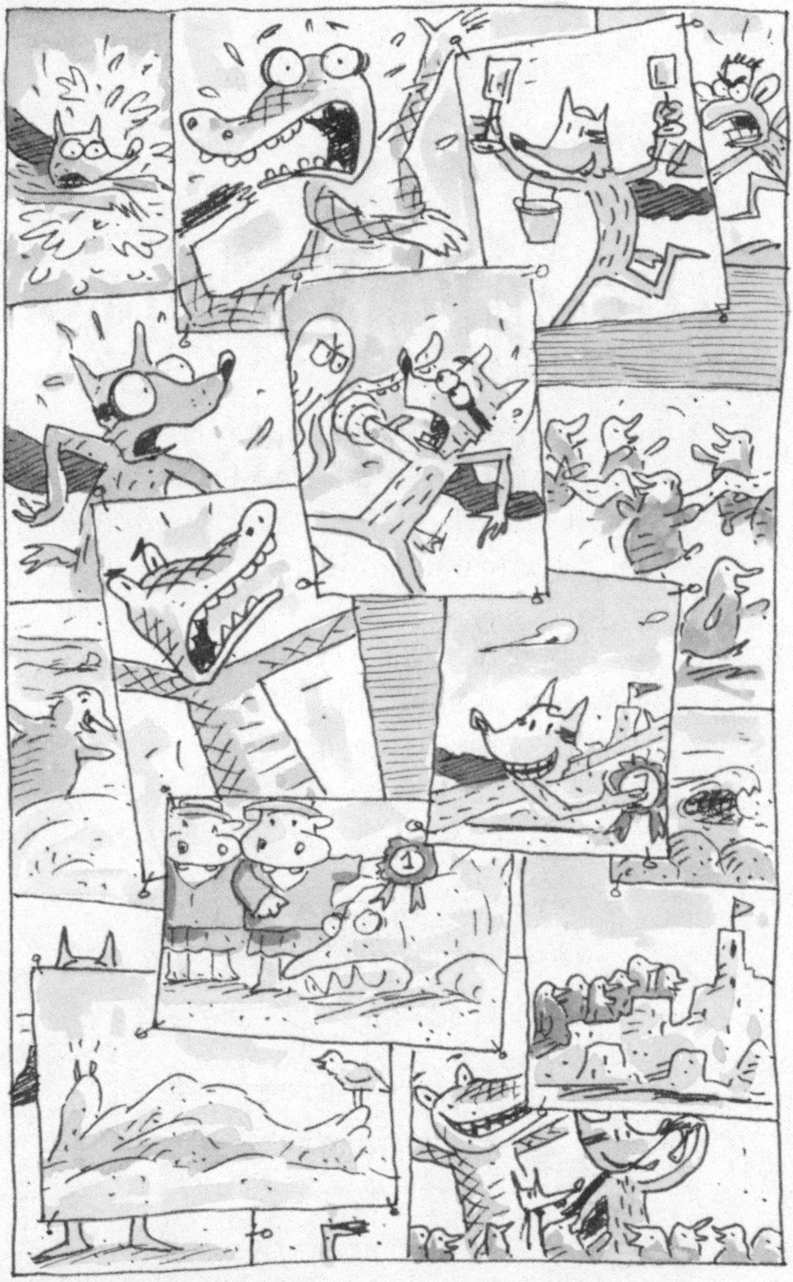

WOMBAT & FOX
BOOK 3

THRILLSEEKERS

Wild and Dangerous Deeds

Fox stood at the door to his
apartment block.
There was a keypad where
the lock used to be.
'What...?'

Fox looked up at Wombat's balcony.
'Help me, Wombat! I'm locked out!'
Wombat trotted downstairs to let him in.

'What happened
to the lock?'
asked Fox.
'We have a new
security system, Foxy.
We don't need a key anymore.'
'So how do we get in?'
'With a password,' said Wombat.
'Any word we like?' asked Fox.
'Any word, Foxy. We just need to pick one.'

'What about *fox*?' suggested Fox.

'Well, that could work,' said Wombat.

'We just need to press the F-O-X letters on the keypad. Just like the numbers and letters on your mobile phone.'

'Okay,' said Fox. 'F is number 3. O is number 6. X is 9. So *fox* is 369.'

'If you say so,' said Wombat. 'But I think it's a bit short.'

'A bit short?'

'Yes, we need a longer pasword; something the Five Monkeys won't guess so easily.

'Oh,' said Fox. 'Like what?'

'966228 is a good one.'

Fox stared at his phone.

And kept staring.

And stared for
a bit longer.

'Hey!' said Fox. 'That spells *wombat.*'

'How about that!' said Wombat.

'It's a good one – easy to remember.'

'So is 369,' said Fox.

'369 is too short!'

'No, it isn't.'

'Yes, it is.'

'Isn't'

'Is.'

'Try 668 3247,' said Fox.

'What's that spell?' asked Wombat.

'*Not fair!*'

'Let's not argue, Wombat. Today is special,'
said Fox.
'You remembered?'
'Sure did! HAPPY BIRTHDAY, WOMBAT!'
'Thank you, Foxy. Is that a birthday present?'
'Well, it *is* wrapped in birthday paper, Wombat.'

Wombat ripped the paper off his present.
'A pen and a notebook!' he cried.
'Just what I wanted.'
Fox beamed.
He loved getting Wombat just what he wanted.

'How did you pay for them?'
'I saved up,' said Fox.

Actually he didn't.
Fox didn't have any money
to save. He found them both
on the newsagent's throw out pile.
The wrapping paper too.

Wombat sat at the table writing in his book.
'Are you writing about me?' asked Fox.
'No, Foxy, why would I do that?'
'No reason.'
'I am sick of boring birthdays,
so I'm making a list of
WILD and DANGEROUS deeds
to do between now and my next birthday.'

'That's a great idea,' said Fox.
'I'm going to do that too.'
So they sat for nineteen minutes and wrote
down all the wild and dangerous deeds they
could think of.

'Finished!' said Wombat.
'Now it's time for some birthday breakfast.'

After he had his birthday porridge
and birthday cup of tea and had
taken his birthday shower and
put on his birthday suit,
Wombat was ready
to go outside.

'Now let's do all the WILD and DANGEROUS deeds on my birthday list,' he said.
'Good idea,' said Fox. 'I've got twelve wild and dangerous deeds on my list.'
'There are one hundred and one on *my* list,' said Wombat.
'Oh dear, Wombat, that's far too many for one day. Let's choose the best three.'

'Number One: Demolish an old building with explosives.'
'Wombat, no one is going to let us use explosives.'

'I guess you're right,' said Wombat.
'What about Number Two: Put my head
in a bear's jaw. That would be dangerous.'
'And just where are we going to find a bear?'
'What about Bear from across the road.'
'Possibly,' said Fox. 'But he is old and has
no teeth. That's hardly wild and dangerous.'

'Okay, Foxy, good point. We could do
Number Three: Jumping out of a plane into
the sea without a parachute.'
'Sharks, Wombat, you know I hate **SHARKS**!'
'Okay, Foxy. What's on your list then?'

'Well,' said Fox. 'We could try getting
out of bed on the wrong side.
Who knows what could happen?'
'That's hardly wild, Foxy.'
'But it is dangerous, Wombat.'

'Forget that.
What's next on your list?'
'Number Two: Rocking back on my chair.
My mum always says it's really dangerous.'
'I'd rather jump out of an aeroplane
without a parachute, Foxy.'

'Okay, Number Three,' said Fox.
'Running with scissors.'
'Running with scissors, Foxy?'
'Really sharp scissors!'

'How about Number Four on my list?'
said Wombat. 'Riding a motorcycle
over a canyon. Now that *is* WILD
and DANGEROUS.'
'And we'll die,' said Fox. 'I don't want to die.'

Wombat checked his list.
'Number Sixty-seven?
Microwaving an egg.'
'We're out of eggs,' said Fox.
'But we've got an avocado.'
'Hardly dangerous,'
said Wombat.

'Number Seventy-eight: Scootering
down Bandicoot's Hill,' said Wombat.
'That sounds like fun.
And we might not die,' said Fox.
'We won't die, Foxy,' said Wombat.
'We might land in the duck pond though.'

'You know what water does to my fur.'
'Okay,' said Wombat. 'We scooter down
Bandicoot's Hill and stop before
the duck pond.'

'So Number Seventy-eight it is then,'
said Wombat.
'I guess so,' said Fox.
'Let's do it!' said Wombat.

Bandicoot's Hill looked
very big and very steep.

It was a quiet Sunday morning.
There were not many pedestrians.
Just the occasional duck.

Wombat looked down the hill.
'Aaahhh!' he beamed. 'The perfect
WILD and DANGEROUS birthday deed.'
'Stupid and insane!' said Fox.
'I'm not scootering down this hill.'
'But it's my birthday, Foxy. I can't do my
wild and dangerous deed on my own.'

Fox took
a deep breath,
closed his eyes,
straightened his cape
and breathed out slowly.
'I'll do it for you, Wombat,'
he said. 'But I'm not getting wet.
I don't want to ruin my new cape!'
'Okay, we'll stay out of the pond,' said Wombat.
'Now here's the deal: I steer and you brake.'
'This scooter has brakes?' said Fox. 'Hooray!'

'When I say "brake", Foxy, you brake.'
'Got it,' said Fox, who repeated it just
to be sure. 'You say "brake", and I brake!'

'And we stop before the duck pond.'
'Of course,' said Fox. 'I DO know how
to ride a scooter, Wombat!'

'Okay, Foxy. Ready.'
Fox stuck up
both thumbs.
'Set.'
Fox nodded.
'GO!'
Wombat scootered.
'Nooo!' cried Fox
as he jumped off.
Wombat braked.

'What happened, Foxy?'
'Sorry, Wombat! If I'm going to do this
wild and dangerous deed, I need protection.'

Fox ran home and returned completely
wrapped in pillows.

'Okay, Foxy, are you ready?'
said Wombat.
'Yep!'
'Set.'
'Set,' repeated Fox.
'GO!!'

'NNOOO!' cried Fox,
jumping off again.

'What is it this time?'
asked Wombat.
'I need my lucky troll,' said Fox.
And he ran back home to get it.

'You got your lucky charm?' asked Wombat.
Fox held up his leg.
'It's on my braking foot,' he said.
'Good idea, Foxy.'

'All set this time, Foxy?'
'Aye, aye, Captain Wombat.'

'Okay, countdown time,' said Wombat.
'Are you sure you don't just want to
step on cracks instead?' asked Fox.

'READY?'
'Ready,' said Fox.
'SET!'
'GO!'
Fox tried to jump off,
but Wombat held him
tight and they scootered
down the hill.

274

'YEAHHH!'
shouted Wombat.
'NOOOOO!' shouted Fox.
'Feel the wind in your fur,' said Wombat.
Fox's cape flew out behind him.
He stood up tall.
'Superfox!' he said under his breath.

Rabbit was halfway across the path,
when she heard a noise and looked up.
Wombat and Fox were hurtling towards her.

She tried to run,
but her feet
wouldn't move.

She tried to scream,
but her voice
wouldn't make
a sound.

Poor Rabbit froze
with fear.

'Watch out, Rabbit!' yelled Fox.
'BRAKE!' said Wombat.
Fox fumbled with his feet.
They wouldn't go where he wanted them to.

'BRAKE!'

cried Wombat.
Fox untangled his feet.

'BRAKE, FOXY!'

Fox pressed hard on the brake pedal.

SCREEEEEECH!!!

They came to a stop
just in front of Rabbit.

'Rabbit! Are you okay?' asked Wombat.
'Milk! Must get milk,' said Rabbit.
She was very confused.
'We'll take you to the shop,'
said Wombat.

'Milk!' was all Rabbit
would say.
So they put her
on the scooter,
and continued down the hill.

'We nearly bumped into her,' said Fox.
'But we didn't,' said Wombat.
'I braked just in time, didn't I?' said Fox.
'That was teamwork, Foxy.'
'And my lucky troll, Wombat.'

As they scootered down the hill,
Rabbit woke from her trance.
She clung to Wombat's fur.
Fox felt the wind ruffle his cape.

'Eeeek!' cried Rabbit.
The Twenty Little Penguins were
crossing the road in front
of the speeding scooter.
The Twenty Penguins made
a long line; too long
a line to go around.
And too high
to go over!

**'Watch out,
Penguins!'**
yelled Fox.

'Brake!' yelled Wombat.
Fox braked as hard as he could.
No foot fumbles this time.
They screeched to a stop in front of the
Penguins, who had gathered into a huddle.

'What's up, Penguins?'
'We're in a hurry.'
'What hurry?'
'Sixteen and Seventeen need to go
  to synchronised swimming classes,'
  said Big Penguin.
'And they're late,' said Nine.
'Very late,' added Twelve.

'Hop aboard, Sixteen and Seventeen,
and we'll take you to the bottom
of the hill,' said Wombat.
They didn't need to be asked twice.
But Wombat asked them twice anyway.
'Come on, Penguins.'

Sixteen and Seventeen
held onto Fox,
and they all scootered
down the hill.

'We're not going to fall into that
duck pond, are we?' said Penguin Seventeen.
'Don't worry, Penguins. We're expert
stoppers, Fox and I.'
And to prove his point,
Wombat gave Fox a wink.
'Brake!' he called.
And Fox slammed
on the brakes.
The scooter came
to a quick stop.

'That's teamwork, Foxy!'
'And my lucky troll, Wombat.'

They continued down the hill.
'I love the feeling of the wind
in my fur,' said Wombat.
'I love the way my cape flaps
out behind me,' said Fox.
'I'm flying,' said Wombat.
'This is WILD and DANGEROUS!'

'Happy birthday, Wombat,' said Fox.

They flew through the roundabout,
over the kerb and onto the jetty.

Fox was ready on the brake.
'Wait for my call, Foxy,' said Wombat.
It was a short jetty.

'BRAKE!'

yelled Wombat.
Fox panicked.
His lucky troll
got stuck under
the brake pedal.

'BRAKE!'

yelled Wombat.

Fox couldn't press the brake pedal!

'BRA

KE!'

Finally Fox kicked his lucky troll
out from under the brake pedal.
He pressed hard.
The brake gripped.
The wheels screeched.
Smoke rose.

The scooter slid across
the jetty, almost to the end.
But at the very last moment,
Fox gave the brake a harder-than-hard
push and the scooter skidded to a stop.

Right at the end of the jetty.
And I mean the VERY end.
Wombat dangled over the water.
The Five Monkeys paddled
by in their blow-up raft.

'Ha! Ha! Look at the big fat fur-ball,'
said the oldest monkey.
'Don't let go, Wombat,'
said the second–oldest monkey.

The scooter was perfectly balanced…
Then Rabbit and the two Little Penguins
jumped off.

The scooter tipped.
'NOOO!' cried the
second-youngest monkey.
'Paddle, brothers!'

Wombat and Fox fell off the jetty and bounced the Five Monkeys off their raft and into the duck pond.

'Fat Wombat falling from the sky,' cried the youngest monkey. 'Swim for your lives, brothers.'

Wombat and Fox floated
off across the duck pond.
'Good braking, Foxy,' said Wombat.
'Good landing, Wombat,' said Fox.
'Best birthday ever,' said Wombat.

Devil's Magic Words

Wombat and Fox stood outside
their apartment block.
'Horse,' said Wombat.
'Giraffe,' said Fox.
'Toaster.'
'Vacuum cleaner.'
'This is hopeless.'

They had forgotten the password
to their security door.
Again!

'We could wake up Moose,' said Wombat.
'Last time we did that, we got him out
of the shower,' said Fox. 'He was **not** happy.'

It was true, Wombat and Fox had locked
themselves out so many times their
neighbours were sick of letting them in.

'We could knock on Toothless Tiger's door.'
'No,' said Wombat. 'Last time he talked to us
for hours; we couldn't get away. We don't
want to go through *that* again.'

They walked around to the side of the
building. 'Our balcony's not so far up,'
said Wombat. 'We could climb.'
'You could,' said Fox. 'I'm not.'
'Come on, Foxy. We could take
it one balcony at a time.'
'Is our balcony door open?' asked Fox.
'I think so,' said Wombat. 'Give me a boost.'

Wombat climbed onto the first balcony.
He reached down and pulled Fox up.

They climbed very quietly onto the
next balcony. They didn't want to wake
Toothless Tiger.

Finally they made it to their own balcony.
The door was locked.
And so was the window.

'What about the roof?' said Wombat.
'What choice do we have?' said Fox.
Wombat boosted Fox up to the roof.

Fox reached down to Wombat.

'You are very heavy, Wombat.
What did you have for breakfast?'

'Just porridge and a banana,' said Wombat.
'And two slices of toast.
And a second helping of porridge.
And an apple. Or two. And some leftover pizza.
And two hard-boiled eggs.'

'Yes, I can tell, Wombat. You are too heavy,'
said Fox.

'Do you need a hand?'
'EEEK!' said Fox. 'Who are you?'
'Devil is the name, helping is the game,'
 said the stranger.

And that is just what he did.
In the blink of an eye, he had
pulled Wombat up onto the roof.

The stranger's full name was *Tasmanian Devil*,
but that was too fancy for him.
He preferred to be called just plain Devil.

'What are you doing up here?'
'Devil has been sleeping on your roof,
under the stars,' he said.
'How did you get in?' asked Fox.
'*We* can't even get in.'
'Devil wanders from rooftop to rooftop
across the city. Yours was such a friendly
rooftop, Devil decided to stay for a while.'

'Well, Devil, come downstairs and we'll make you a thank-you snack.'

Fox tried the door to the stairwell.
It was locked.

'Small matter, comrades,' said Devil.
He reached behind his ear and took
out a hairpin, which he slid into the lock.
He jiggled it about and whispered some
mysterious words.
The lock opened.

'Wow,' said Fox. 'That was like magic.'
'That's right, Fox,' he said. 'It's all in the words.'

Wombat growled. 'Huh, magic words indeed!'

Fox set out some milk and bread.
'Devil is very hungry, Fox.
Keep the bread coming,' said Devil.

Meanwhile, Wombat read
through the list he had made of
WILD and DANGEROUS deeds.

Fox sat on the balcony, sweltering in the heat.
Devil was still hungry.
So was Fox.
And Wombat too.
'Let Devil make you a treat,' said Devil.

Devil made pancakes.
He flipped them into the air and
caught them in the frying pan.

'That's clever,' said Fox.
Devil threw one right across the room.
It landed on Fox's plate.

'Let me try,' said Fox.
He flipped the pancake and it flew up in the air, but it didn't come down. It got stuck on the ceiling.

He tried again,
but the next one fell
on Wombat's head.

'You need the magic words,'
said Devil, and he whispered to Fox.

When the next pancake was ready to flip,
Fox repeated Devil's magic words.
Flipiddy diddle
Flipiddy dee
Flip this pancake
Back to me.

And, sure enough, when Fox flipped the
pancake, it did a somersault and flopped
right back into the pan.

'Did you see that, Wombat!
Devil taught me how to flip a pancake.'
'Great, Foxy,' said Wombat and returned
to his birthday list.

'There are still lots of deeds on my WILD
and DANGEROUS list,' said Wombat.
'I want to go to the swimming pool.'
'Okay,' said Fox and Devil together.
'We can try Number Eighty-eight:
The high-diving tower,' said Wombat.

'Towels.'
'Check!'

'Sunscreen.'
'Check!'

'Sunnies and hats.'
'Double check!'

'Ready!'

On the way to the pool,
Devil climbed up onto a low wall
and balanced his way along it.
Wombat was good at balancing, too.
Fox scrambled up, but fell straight off.

'Steady, comrade, try Devil's words.'
He whispered into Fox's ear.

Fox hopped up onto the wall.
Flipiddy diddle
Flipiddy dee
I'm on the wall
And the wall's under me.

Fox wobbled a few times and then
walked confidently along the wall.
'Thank you, Devil,' he said.

All three friends walked along the wall,
until Mouse scampered across their path.
She spooked Fox.
He fell off the wall.

The swimming pool was a wide, round, deep
bend in the river, with a swinging rope and
a high-diving tower.

Wombat, Fox and Devil dived into the cool water. Then they warmed up on the grass in the sun. And when they got too hot, they dived into the water again.

'It's time,' said Wombat.
'What time?' asked Fox.
'3:41,' said Wombat.
'So?'
'It's time for the high-diving tower.
Are you coming?'
'Me?' said Fox. 'Are you kidding?'
'Devil is in, Wombat.
And so is comrade Fox.'
'I am?'
'You are.'
'Oh,' said Fox.

They climbed up
the thirty-two steps
to the first level.

'This will do,' said Fox.
'No,' said Wombat. 'It has to be WILD and
DANGEROUS. We have to go to the top.'
They climbed the final steps to the very top.
All three crept to the edge of the tower.
'Hmmm,' said Wombat.
'Gosh,' said Devil.
'ARRRGGGHHH!!' said Fox.

'I am a wombat of WILD
and DANGEROUS deeds,'
said Wombat and he leapt
off the tower.

SPLASH!
Devil followed close
behind Wombat.

SPLASH!

They waited, but there was no third splash.

The Five Monkeys climbed the tower.
'Hurry up, Fox,' said the oldest monkey.
'You're holding up everyone else.'

'Just jump, scaredy-cat!'
  said the middle monkey.

'I don't think I want to jump either,'
  said the youngest monkey.

Wombat and Devil climbed back to
the top of the tower. Wombat growled
at the Five Monkeys.

'Jump!' said Devil.

And he bared his teeth.
He had a very impressive set of sharp fangs.
The monkeys didn't stay around
to find out *how* sharp.
All together they jumped.

Even the youngest monkey.

SPLASH!
SPLASH!
SPLASH!
SPLASH!
SPLASH!

'Now, Foxy,' said Wombat. 'Let's try again.'
Fox said nothing.

Wombat took a close look at his friend.
Fox was frozen with fear.
Not *cold* frozen.
Not just *couldn't-move* frozen.
But *frozen-to-the-spot* frozen.

Wombat shook Fox gently.

He tapped him on the cheek.
Fox didn't flinch.

Devil blew in Fox's ear.
He didn't even blink.

'Comrade Fox. I know
you can hear Devil.
He's going to give
you a little song
to break you out of this spell.'
Devil whispered into Fox's ear:
Flipiddy diddle
Flipiddy dee
Forget your fear
And look at me.

But Fox stayed frozen.

Wombat and Devil stayed with Fox
at the top of the high-diving tower.
Every now and then they tried something new.
A pinch.
A tweak of the nose.
A tickle.
A poke.
But nothing worked.

Fox was stuck on top of the high-diving tower
frozen with fear all through the afternoon.

Elephant suggested they splash water
on Fox. She let him have a whole trunk full,
but it had no effect.

Croc suggested they stand
Fox in a bucket of water.
That did no good either.

The Twenty Little Penguins suggested
they all peck him.
'That will surely wake him,'
said Big Penguin.
But it didn't.

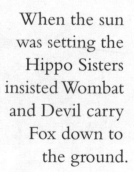

When the sun
was setting the
Hippo Sisters
insisted Wombat
and Devil carry
Fox down to
the ground.

But getting Fox down the
very steep steps was too difficult.

'Devil has an idea,' said Devil.
'Move Comrade Fox to the edge
and everybody stand back.'

Devil stood just behind Fox and
whispered another song into his ear.

Then with a great big shove,
Devil pushed Fox off the tower.

'AARRGGGHHHH!!!'

SPLASH!

'Help, Wombat!'
cried Fox.
'Swim!' shouted Devil.
'I can't believe you pushed
him off!' said Wombat.

They hurried down the tower
and pulled Fox out of the water.
'Are you crazy!' said Fox.

'When nothing else will
work, sometimes we just
need a good push.'
'I could have died!'
'Well, you didn't. Devil knows best.'

'I'm not so sure about that,' said Wombat.

Fox was too exhausted to walk home, so
Wombat and Devil took turns carrying him.

Only they couldn't get past the security door.
'We forgot to change the password,'
said Wombat.

'Allow me,' said Devil.
He placed his head
next to the keypad.

He closed his
eyes and pressed
a few buttons.

He sang one of his
little songs and the
door swung open.

'Truly magical, Devil,' said Fox.
Even Wombat was impressed.

The next morning, when Fox ran
up to the rooftop to offer him breakfast,
Devil was gone.

'His kind are always on the move,'
said Wombat.
'But I thought he was my friend.'
'He is, Foxy. He's your
always-on-the-move friend.'

'Now sit down and have a pancake.
It's a Wombat-special.'

Superfox Saves the Day

'Look!' said Wombat.

'There's our apartment.'

'I can't see it,' said Fox.

'That's because you have your eyes closed, Foxy.'

'That's because we are very high, Wombat.'

'You're not kidding,' said Croc.
'The Five Monkeys look like ants.'
'I wish they were ants,' said Fox.
'If you think this Ferris wheel is high,
 wait till you ride the Roller-coaster, Foxy.'

'I'm not ready for the Roller-coaster,'
 said Fox. 'Let's try the Teacups first.'

The teacup rose gently and the whole
ride turned slowly.
'See, Wombat, this is my kind of ride.'
Fox sat back with his arms resting
on the lip of the cup.
'I can even keep my eyes open!'

The ride began to turn faster.
Fox shut his eyes.

Then the inside of their
teacup started spinning.
Fox turned white.
'Wombat!' cried Fox. 'I think
my head is about to come off.'
'Just hang on to it, Foxy,' said Wombat.

Fox held on to his head very tightly.
It didn't come off.
But his eyes nearly popped
out of their sockets.
When the ride stopped,
Fox was very giddy.
'I feel sick,' he said.

'Let's try the merry-go-round, Foxy,' said
Wombat. 'I think it will be more your speed.'
Fox stared at the horses.
Most had wild eyes
and crazy
mouths.

Finally he found one with sleepy eyes
and a smiley mouth.
The merry-go-round moved
very slowly indeed.
'This is perfect,' said Fox.
'Boring,' said Croc.
'I agree,' said Wombat.
'Let's try the Roller-
coaster next.'

They lined up at the Roller-coaster.
'It's so high I can't even see the top,' said Croc.
'No way,' said Fox. 'I'm not riding
the Roller-coaster.'
'But, Foxy!' said Wombat.
'I don't want to die,' said Fox.

'Ha! Ha! Fox is too scared to ride the Roller-
coaster,' said the oldest of the Five Monkeys.
'We heard you won free tickets,'
said the second-oldest monkey.
'Yes,' said Croc. 'I did win tickets.'
'If Fox is too scared to use them,
you should give us some of your tickets,'
said the middle monkey.
'No way!' said Croc.

'But sharing is caring,'
said the second-youngest monkey.
'When have you ever shared anything
with us?' asked Wombat.
'I gave you a cold once,'
said the youngest monkey.

Wombat, Fox and Croc ducked in to the
Tunnel of Love and climbed into a boat.

The Five Monkeys snuck in and piled into
the next boat. They are very good sneakers.

They splashed Wombat, Fox and Croc,
and threw chewed chewing gum at them.
They tried to spook them with ghost noises.
Fox knelt at the very back of their boat,
leaned out over the edge and tried
to splash them back.

Croc held tight to his cape so he didn't fall.
'Good splashing, Foxy,' said Wombat.

When the ride was finished, Wombat, Fox and Croc leaped out of the boat and ran as far away from the Five Monkeys as possible.

'Let's go on the Roller-coaster now,' said Wombat. 'Quick, while *you-know-who* aren't around.

'No,' said Fox. 'I told you, I am NOT ready for the Roller-coaster.'

So they rode the Dodgem Cars.

It didn't take long for the Five Monkeys to catch up with them. They snuck onto the ride and all squeezed into one of the empty cars.

They zoomed up behind Fox.

He turned right.
They turned right.

He turned left.
They turned left.

Then they crashed into him

THUMP!

'OWWCCHH!!' cried Fox.
'MY neck!! I think I have whiplash!'

'LEAVE MY FRIEND ALONE!'
cried Croc, and she drove her car straight
at the Five Monkeys.

BUMP!

With one mighty bump she pushed the
Five Monkeys right off the ride.

'No bumping!'

yelled the two Hippo Sisters.
They were the ride attendants and
they had very sparkly red uniforms.

'Leave the ride immediately!'

The Five Monkeys' car rolled down the hill
towards the House of Horrors.

The Hippo Sisters
chased Wombat,
Fox and Croc, but
our friends hid
behind the hot
food stands.

'Your stomach is rumbling, Wombat,'
said Fox. 'The Hippo Sisters will hear it.'
'I can't help it,' said Wombat.
'I smell doughnuts.'

'Attention. Thrillseekers Park
is closing in ten minutes.'
'What!' said Fox. 'That's
not fair! We only just
got here.'

'Riding the Roller-coaster is on my birthday
list of WILD and DANGEROUS deeds,'
said Wombat.
'But the park is closing,' said Fox.
'We have to go home.'

'*WE* are not going anywhere,' said the oldest
monkey. 'We're hiding until everyone leaves.'
'Then we will have the park all to ourselves,'
said the second–oldest monkey.

'I am staying too, Foxy,' said Wombat.
'I REALLY want to ride that Roller-coaster.
It's Number Eighty-eight on my list.'

'Come on, Foxy,' said Wombat. 'It'll be fun.'

Fox took a deep breath.
He tightened his mask and shook out his cape.
'I am Superfox,' he said. 'I will stay.'

Wombat, Fox, Croc and the Five Monkeys
hid in the House of Horrors.

They waited.

And waited.

The park staff turned off the power, rolled
down the big shutters and left for the night.

'HOORAY! We have the place to ourselves,' said the Five Monkeys.

Wombat, Fox and Croc played on the rolling barrels. They laughed at each other's reflections in the trick mirrors.

When the Five Monkeys were sure the staff
had gone far, far away, they opened the power
box and switched on all the rides.

'I have a bad feeling about this, Wombat.'
'Relax, Foxy. It's time for WILD and
DANGEROUS deeds.'
'Remember, you are Superfox,' said Croc.

All three crowded into
one of the Roller-coaster cars.

It started slowly then climbed a steep slope.
Fox gripped hard on the safety bar.

As they rolled to the top,
he closed his eyes.
They flew down the slope.
Fox screamed.

Wombat and Croc threw their arms in the air.
They stuck out their tongues.
Croc's long tongue flapped in the breeze.

They reached the bottom
and flew up the next slope,
to the very top.

'Look, Foxy,' said Wombat. 'I can see the beach.'
Fox's eyes were shut tighter than ever.

When Wombat, Fox and Croc were at the
very highest point of the Roller-coaster,
the car suddenly jerked to a stop.

'What happened?' asked Fox.

'Ha! Ha! Ha!' said the Five Monkeys from
below. 'We turned the power off.'
'Guess where you are spending the night,'
yelled the second-oldest monkey.
'Let us down,' yelled Fox.
'Sleep well,' yelled all Five Monkeys as they
clambered over the fence and ran home.

Wombat and Croc gazed out
across the lights of the city as night fell.
Fox's eyes were still closed.

'Wombat, call for help,' said Fox.
'Good idea, Foxy.'
Wombat fiddled with his phone,
then put it away.
'Well?' said Fox.
'Battery's flat!'
'This is a disaster!'
said Fox.

'We can't spend the night up here,' said Fox.
'Why not?' said Wombat. 'It's a very WILD
and DANGEROUS deed. If I'd thought of it,
I would have put it on my list.'

'Croc?' said Fox.
'Could you climb down
 and get help?'

'And food,' said Wombat.
'No problem for Croc,' she said.
'I can slide down the rails.'
'You'll get splinters,' said Wombat.

Croc climbed out of the
car and onto the frame
of the Roller-coaster.

'Uh-oh,' said Croc.
'I think I'm stuck.'

'Are you all right, Croc?' called Fox.
There was no answer.

Wombat leaned over the edge of the car and
looked down. 'I think she's fallen asleep, Foxy.'

'This is a disaster,' said Fox.

'It's not a disaster, Foxy,' said Wombat. 'This is
the best WILD and DANGEROUS deed ever.'

'I'm still not opening my eyes.'
'Go on, Foxy. The view is brilliant.'
'Not listening.'
'Full moon reflecting on the water.'
'Still not listening.'
'Fireworks over the city.'
'Laa dee daaa! Laa laa!'

There was a long silence.

'We could write a note and make it into
a paper plane and throw it.'

'We have no paper,'
said Wombat.

'We could jump up and
down and yell for help.
Someone would see us.'

'There is no one about.'

'We could make my cape into a parachute. That's it! Wombat, what do you think of that for an idea?'

'Wombat?'

'Wombat?'

'Wombat?'

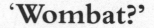

Fox sighed. Wombat had fallen into a deep sleep. Such a deep snoring sleep that nothing would wake him.

So poor Fox spent a sleepless night on the highest point of the Roller-coaster, and he never opened his eyes. Not even a tiny peek. Not once.

In the early hours of the morning,
a voice called to him.
'Hello, comrade.'
'Devil, is that you?'
said Fox.

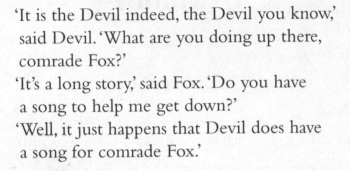

'It is the Devil indeed, the Devil you know,'
said Devil. 'What are you doing up there,
comrade Fox?'
'It's a long story,' said Fox. 'Do you have
a song to help me get down?'
'Well, it just happens that Devil does have
a song for comrade Fox.'

'Flipiddy dee,
Flipiddy ache,
The way to get down,
Is to take off the brake.'

'The brake!'
said Fox.

'What brake?'

He felt around his seat.
Sure enough,
he found a lever.

'Thank you, Devil!' he called,
but Devil had disappeared.

Fox opened his eyes. He blinked.
He looked down the Roller-coaster track.
'Very steep,' he whispered.

'I am Superfox,'
he said quietly.

One more look
down the track.
It was still steep.

Fox took a big breath and released the brake.
The Roller-coaster car rolled slowly at first,
but soon it was hurtling down the track.
The wind blew through Fox's fur.
His cape fluttered behind him.
Fox stood.
He stretched out his arms.
'I am king of the world!'

The Roller-coaster flew down, then up to
the top of the next peak. It rattled on, up and
down and up and down all the way to the
station, where it rolled to a gentle stop.

Fox shook Wombat.
'Wake up, sleepy head,' he said.
'Superfox has saved the day!'

And so he had.

A Message From
Terry Denton

Wombat and Fox have frenemies
known as the Five Monkeys,
because there are five of them,
and they are all monkeys.
I grew up in a family of five –
boys, not monkeys (although it
was hard to tell sometimes).
So, I know how Fox feels.
The Five Monkeys never really
pick on Wombat, but they do torment Fox.
One to tease him.
One to poke him.
One to pinch him.
One to choke him.
And the youngest monkey is just relieved that
they are no longer picking on him.

So, why am I hanging here all tied up with rope?
Well, that's another story.
The Five Monkeys could
explain, but I am not
talking to them.